DEVIOUS BELOVED

USA TODAY BESTSELLING AUTHOR
T.L. SMITH

DEDICATION

*To all my devious book lovers out there, I hope he shows
you what a good "bunny" you could be if you just got on
your knees.*

Devious Beloved by T.L. Smith

WARNING

This book contains sexually explicit scenes and adult language and may be considered offensive to some readers. This book is intended for adults ONLY. Please store your book wisely, where they cannot be accessed by under-aged readers.

BLURB

He's devious, and my soon to be husband.

I didn't choose him.

I was coerced.

Whiskey has a way of manipulating me. He knows
I'll do whatever it takes to protect my family.

He's found my weakness and he's exploiting it.

Seizing as he sees as his opportunity.

Now, I'm his wife for the next year.

I'm counting down the days until my time is up.

Until I'm free.

However, it doesn't seem to matter how devious he
is, or the fact he's my father's friend.

When he's near, I want him to stay.

I hate how I love being married to my devious
husband.

CHAPTER 1
WHISKEY

He screams as my foot applies more pressure.

"Whiskey."

I ignore Barry as he pulls at my arms, but I shake him off. He wants me to leave. I want to leave as well. At least I *think* I should want to leave. But first...

As I press my foot down further, his screams grow even louder. It's like music to my ears.

My life has been hell, and inflicting pain on others has been a release from the torment that has been eating away at me.

"He doesn't want him dead, Whiskey." Barry tries to pull me away again. But the screams from John at my feet tell me he's about to give me what I want.

"You've had a change of heart, haven't you?" I ask him. He nods, and I smile, pressing down one last time as his screams fill the rest of the room. I turn to Barry and give him a smug grin I hope conveys *I fucking told you.*

"You'll break his cock, Whiskey. Fuck. Come on, man." Barry winces as he takes a step back, obviously feeling the phantom pains of what I'm inflicting on John. Barry has always been fine with me shooting a man and breaking legs, but because of where my foot is, he's uncomfortable. The crunching sound his cock makes when my foot applies pressure does make me cringe too—just a little.

"I'll do it. I'll back him. I'll do whatever. Just please," he pleads. I release my foot from his cock, and he instantly cups it with his hands. Bitch. He won't be safe until I get what I want out of him.

I bend down so we're eye to eye.

"If you mention this to anyone…" I nod to where his hand is. "I'll come back and finish the job." I stand and walk out, Barry hot on my heels as we reach the car. He doesn't speak as we drive.

"You need to stop doing his dirty work," Barry says, his hands on the steering wheel.

"I will."

"Whiskey, man, you are richer than him. Richer

than any man I know. You don't need the money, so why?"

"It's an outlet." And that's as much as I can tell him. We stop at the senator's house. It's dark but I know they're home. The cars are all parked in the driveway. I get out just as the front door flies open, and she runs out. It may have been a few years since I last saw her, but I would recognize her anywhere.

His daughter. I should hate her on principal. I hate him.

I watch as she pulls on a hat, her red locks hiding under it. She doesn't see me at first, but I step closer. It's as if she's trying to escape, to where I don't know. But she clearly doesn't want to be seen.

She walks directly in my path—clearly more worried about looking at the house, rather than her surroundings—not watching at all and she smacks straight into me.

"Oh, my god! Oh, shit." Her hands touch my chest. "I'm so sorry. I was…" She points over her shoulder as she looks back to me, and her green eyes lock onto me. This is no longer the young girl that used to follow her father and me around the grounds. I try remembering her age, then I recall the invitation last month— the invitation to her eighteenth birthday party. "Look, can you please not tell him? He thinks I'm sleeping, and I would rather him not know. Please?" I say nothing as I watch her mouth move. She's a pretty little thing. But too young.

Too young.

I'm almost thirty; even looking at an eighteen-year-old sounds wrong. But in this moment, I can't look away from those emerald orbs that are practically pleading with me.

"Do you speak?" she asks, and a hint of a smirk touches my lips. "Fine, whatever. Just don't tell him." She pulls down on her hat and steps around me. I watch as she runs down the driveway and out to the road where a car waits for her. She climbs in, and I exhale. I was here to tell the senator the job is done. But honestly, now I don't care to tell him anything. Instead, I go back to the car and climb in. It's time to make a change, and the first part is to stop doing his dirty work.

This night, I dream of a little redhead.

CHAPTER 2
LOTTIE
SEVEN YEARS LATER.

"*T**his isn't going to work, take your ring back.*"

It's been weeks since I ended my engagement.

It was the smart thing to do.

I didn't love him, even if my father did.

His kisses were dry, his hands were always cold. And the way he looked at me made my skin crawl. I couldn't imagine having to spend my days with a man like him.

He was marrying me for one reason and one reason only: my father.

And my father doesn't take no for an answer—even from his own daughter.

His words echo in the back of my mind.

Date Colton! He's a nice boy.

You should marry the boy. He's good for you, and you will do this family proud.

My father doesn't agree with my lifestyle, and like any powerful father, he always has some stupid things to say about the way I live my life.

But somewhere along the way, I started to not care. To rebel. Little bit by little bit.

I went and got my arm tattooed.

Quit college to work at a bar.

But in the end, he still won—because as often as I rebelled, I also gave in to his demands.

I despise the fact I can't say no. Can't be in control of my own life. Until now.

I contemplate this as I take another pull of tequila. It almost makes me choke as I continue to hold it to my lips.

For some strange, fucked-up reason, I ended up at a house party.

Is that even a thing anymore?

Emma said it was a housewarming.

Housewarming for what? Are we meant to warm the fucking house?

"Oh, my god, Lottie! At least chase it with a lime to kill the taste." Emma takes the bottle from my hand, and I shake my head at her.

Does she not know I am trying to drown out the

images of my ex? The least of my worries is how it tastes.

"This isn't the right thing to do, and you know it. You'll wake up tomorrow, and it will all be different."

That was weeks ago, and his voice rings in my head as if I'll change my mind.

How about…no.

"Lottie!" Emma yells at me.

She's been my best friend since I managed to escape my parents' house and start living my own life—well, partial life.

"What? You made me come. Who even has house parties at our age? We aren't teenagers anymore. Fucking hell!" I shake my head and walk away from her.

I'm not mad at Emma. I'm mad at life, and why the hell did I even agree to come here in the first place? The last week or so I have been on my couch, watching horror films and eating all the best foods. I've also been hiding from my father's calls because he is extremely disappointed I broke off the engagement.

"Lottie." I hear Emma's voice, but I wave her off. Walking to the door, I bypass people dancing in the lounge room right next to pristine, white furniture. Talk about a bad set up, especially since these idiots have pink fruity drinks in their hand.

I step outside, and the cool air hits my skin. I'm dressed in a short leather skirt, a black and white polka dot shirt, and I have Doc Martens on my feet. My red hair is tied up in a bandana in a curly mess, and it only completes the overall vibe I'm going for. Stepping off the balcony, I walk farther out. Emma and I took an Uber, and even though I don't want to leave her alone, my desire to be here is waning by the minute.

"Do you live here?" I turn to the sound of the voice—it's rich and dark.

Almost familiar in a way.

The houses are over-the-top. Three-story mansions all built too close together. It seems weird since the rich and famous usually demand their privacy. I mean, if I were paying millions for a home I sure as shit wouldn't want my neighbors hearing me fuck.

But this is the lifestyle I know. My father is very successful. Rich beyond measure. And his lifestyle is ostentatious, which means I was raised in a neighborhood similar to this one.

"Do you live here?" the voice asks again, catching me off guard. But I can't see him.

I hear the rustling of leaves as he moves closer. A huge guy moves out from behind one of the trees on the border of the house. I should be worried.

Shouldn't I? Here I am, standing outside of a party, and no one else is out here except for this man. A man who is stepping closer to me.

"I know how to fight," I randomly say. Damn, that sounded tougher in my head. But I know it didn't work when I hear the slight cackle from the man as he takes another step closer.

"You can? And what training do you have?" he asks. The lights from the house haven't hit him yet, so I still can't see him clearly, but the close proximity has goosebumps breaking out on my arms.

And why do I know that voice?

"A lot. Martial arts, mainly. But other things too."

"You don't know the names of the other things, do you?" Damn him, he caught me.

"I totally do. Boxing," I throw out. He doesn't have to know the extent of my boxing abilities is a summer bootcamp class I took my first semester of college. And I failed miserably at it.

"Yes, okay, sure."

We both go quiet, but I keep my eyes trained on him as he steps closer. The light from the front porch finally begins to reveal the man from the shadows—his bare feet first, followed by his black track suit pants, the way they hug his thick thighs…

When did I become attracted to thighs? As I take in his torso, I realize he isn't wearing a shirt. His toned, tanned, hairy—but not overly, more like Henry Cavill—chest is on display. I don't realize I am ogling him until he stops in front of me, and my eyes find his.

"Lottie," he says.

Oh shit, I do know him.

"Whiskey," I say on a shallow breath. He smirks and the corner of his lip pulls up, and I'm reminded of my teenage crush on him. I'm twenty-five now, and it's been seven years since I last saw him. His presence shouldn't be affecting me this way—not after all these years.

I thought I got over it, but my hands start to sweat, and my heartbeat picks up at just the sight of him.

"Is this your place?"

I shake my head, and he looks past me to the house. I take the seconds to admire his features. His hair, almost mocha in color, is cut shorter than I remember. His sharp jawline is sculpted to perfection, and a light amount of stubble adorns it. That's when my eyes find his lips. The lips I've dreamed about. Damn, he's gorgeous.

"No."

It's all I manage to breathe out. His close proximity limits my ability to speak coherently.

Whiskey is my father's friend. I briefly met him when I was maybe fifteen. He had just started working for my father. I only saw him around every now and then.

"How old are you?" I ask him, I never really asked before but had always been curious. But he doesn't look as old as my father, who is now in his sixties.

His eyes turn to find mine. They remind me of whiskey in a glass, fitting really.

"Thirty-eight," he answers as his eyes continue to roam over me.

"Why aren't you home? I heard you were engaged." His eyes flick down to my hand.

"No, not engaged," I tell him, lifting my empty hand. Before I can lower it, he reaches out, grasping my wrist. His fingers move over the ink on my wrist.

"Last time I saw you, you were a good girl. Now here you stand, dressed in leather, and covered in ink. What happened to you, Lottie? I bet Daddy isn't pleased." His words shock me.

I pull my hand free, and when I do, I see a glimpse of something. What it is exactly, I have no idea. But a part of me can't wait to find out.

"Pleasing my father doesn't seem to be in the cards for me. Especially when disappointment is a common feeling my father harbors for me. I didn't play his pawn and go through with the wedding, so he's not very happy," I say, and want to take the words back the minute they are out.

"I'm sure you know exactly how to *please*." He emphasizes the please in his statement. And his words feel dirty, the best kind of dirty.

"Do you live around here?" I ask, nodding behind him. When I bring my eyes back to him, I can't help but track them down his abs again. "Where's your shirt?"

"I was about to work out, but the noise." He nods back to the house. The party hasn't calmed at all. "Why are you here?"

"I'm rebelling." I smile.

"Interesting," he murmurs.

"If you say so." I smile. And when I do, I know tonight, something just changed for me.

In more ways than one.

CHAPTER 3
LOTTIE

"You should invite me in for a drink." The words leave my mouth before I can stop them. He raises a perfect brow and locks eyes with mine.

"Do you think that's wise, kid?" He always used to call me *kid* when he came over. I assumed it was because he didn't know my name, but now I'm thinking it was something else entirely.

"Do I look like a kid to you?" I ask as I step backward, spinning around in a circle. When I stop moving, my hands fall to my hips, and I look him dead in the eyes.

His eyes slowly trail over my body as I twirl, and something heated passes over his expression. He reaches over and stops me.

"No, you certainly don't look like a kid." A

smile tugs on my lips as he turns without saying a word and stalks back to his house.

I don't budge, confused. That is until he stops and yells over his shoulder.

"Come on woman, let's go!"

I falter at his words but follow him, the leaves crunching under my boots. He stays a few strides ahead of me but stills when he reaches the front door, and holds it open for me. I step in and stop, seeing white marble flooring as I look down at my docs.

"Should I take my shoes off?"

"Yes." He drops down in a crouching position, and his hand comes up and reaches for the back of my calf. *What is he doing?* He lifts it, placing one boot on his thigh as he starts to undo the lace. I'm too stunned to form words, so I settle by following his lead.

Not once has he looked up my skirt, which in his position, he could easily see from his vantage point I am not wearing any underwear. I want him to look, and I am also really hoping he no longer sees me as the *kid* he once knew but a woman standing in front of him. When he pulls off the boot, I see a small smile form on his lips, and he lets out a laugh just as he reaches for my other foot.

"What's funny?" I ask him.

"Your socks have bunnies on them."

"I like bunnies," I tell him. "It's the ears, you know. Cute."

He pulls the second off and stands, and unfortunately, he doesn't look up my skirt. I kind of wish he did.

"Cute." Those are not the words I was hoping for. Cute is not sexy. And cute is not how I want Whiskey picturing me. He turns and walks off into his house, not waiting for me to reply.

"But I thought we came here for a drink," I tell him.

"I think you have had enough to drink," he says with authority.

"Is that so? What if I want more?" My hand goes to my hip, and his eyes fall to my hand.

"It's not going to happen," he says. "You're welcome to join me."

"Join you for what?" I step closer to him, and his eyes track my movements. But when I reach him, he turns to the door behind him and pulls it open.

"In here."

My heart rate picks up. I'm not sure if it's the alcohol or excitement. He's taking me to his bedroom. I mean, that's what I want, right?

I step in, and rock music fills my ears. He walks

straight to a bench and sits down on it, looking over at me. I look around, and a part of me is disappointed. This is not his bedroom. It's his gym.

"I'm sure your father wouldn't approve of you being in my house." My head lolls to the side as one hand falls to my hip.

"Why?" I ask.

He lies back on the bench, and his arms move as he reaches for the work-out bar above his head. I watch him do chest presses and realize the bar has to weigh as much as I do. I wonder if he could lift me like that.

I'd like him to lift me straight onto his face.

Shit.

I've really had too much to drink.

"Because good girls like you shouldn't be around monsters like me."

"I don't see a monster." I walk over to him. My leg brushes his and tingles all the way to my stomach explode at the small contact. I don't touch him with any other part of me. When I look down at him, I see how much he wants me. He may hide it very well, but I can see it hidden in those eyes.

"This is a dangerous game you are playing."

As he says the words, I can see the need, or better yet, the *want*, lingering in his eyes. He sets the bar back in place and sits up, and the action places his eyes level with my chest. Our bodies are so close if he leaned forward his lips would touch my nipples.

And I think I want him to do that.

Yes, I definitely want him to do that.

"Sometimes danger is what we need." I smirk, leaning down so our faces are close. "Are you single?" I ask him.

"But what about that fiancé of yours? What's his name?"

"Clinton? Let's just say I was tired of pretending with him. So, I called it off."

He smirks and before any other words can leave my mouth, he lifts his hand, reaches into my red hair, and pulls my face to his. I feel his grip tighten on my hair as our lips touch.

Kissing.

It's such a funny thing.

I hardly kissed Clinton, and when I did, I felt like it was kissing a ragdoll. It was boring. No sparks, and I hated it.

But with Whiskey, kissing is otherworldly. It feels like he is trying to take my fucking soul. His lips are soft, but also rough with need at the same time. The hand that has my hair is holding on for dear life. When I reach out for him, I come into contact with his bare skin, and there's nothing to latch on to. I slide my hands down as I open my mouth, and that's all the invitation he needs before he slips his tongue in and grips my hair a little harder as I clasp onto his waistband of his pants.

We stay connected, kissing for what feels like ages. I need more. Moving my hand lower, I step back a fraction—never breaking the kiss— so I can slide my hand fully into his pants, grasping his hard cock in my hand.

There is a small part of me saying I should step away. Stop before this goes too far.

I should not be doing this; what would happen if my father found out? Not only is he my father's friend, he is also older than me.

But I won't. I don't want to stop. My hand wraps around him, and as it does, he breaks the kiss, pulling back but not moving. His eyes lock onto mine.

"You should go." His words may say one thing, but his actions say another. His hand is still in my hair, and my hand is still in his pants.

"I should," I agree.

Neither of us move.

I drop to my knees and free his cock, and the minute it's free, my tongue darts out and I lick the tip. He growls, and it's like music to my ears as I take him in. He pushes into my mouth until I'm gagging. Tears begin to pool in my eyes, but the sound he's making urges me on.

But then, he suddenly stops.

"Are you drunk?" he asks. I pull back and fall to my ass. Managing to stand, I draw back to look at him. I'm deciding whether I should tell him the truth or just pretend I haven't drank anything, because I'm worried he may stop if I say I've been drinking.

"Maybe tipsy." I shrug, going with the truth.

He nods and we stand there, my green eyes boring into him. "Have you been drinking?" I ask him.

"Sober as the fucking day I was born," he forces out, obviously still trying to catch his breath. I love knowing the effect I have on him. I know he isn't ready for this to end.

And I love it.

I offer him a slow smile as I reach for my leather skirt zipper. I shimmy it down my bare legs before I unhook my polka dot top and let it fall to the floor, all while he watches me. His eyes trace over every part of my body as I stand there—completely naked.

"Should we…" I wave a hand, and before I can even finish my sentence, he's in front of me and reaching for me. He lifts me up, and I wrap both legs around his waist as he turns me around and positions me on the bench he was just lifting on. His body moves from mine, and he drops to his knees. Before I can even utter a sound or ask him what he is doing, his mouth is on me. My legs spread, and his hot mouth is on my clit. He wastes no time as he starts a slow and steady rhythm. I'm not sure if it's the alcohol or just him, but my hands reach for my breasts, and I grip them—hard. "Don't you fucking stop," I tell him, arching my back.

He doesn't.

He keeps the same rhythm and slides a finger straight into me, then another. He works me over, his mouth only ever leaving for a second, and then he's back to devouring me as if I'm his favorite meal.

What a funny thought.

I lost my virginity when I was seventeen. It was at a party I'd snuck out to. It wasn't fun, actually. Sex and I haven't been the best of friends. Men always seem to want to please themselves first. I thought maybe it would be different with my ex, but it was terrible, and I never want to have that type of sex again in my life.

"Whiskey." I say his name as I come, and I fucking come hard. He moves, and before I can ask him where he's going, he growls.

"Do not fucking move an inch."

I don't even get a chance to nod at his command before he leaves. I try to catch my breath as I hear his footsteps, and before I know it, he's back. I look at him to see him with no pants on and rolling a condom on his very hard cock, the very same one that was in my hand—and mouth—just moments ago. He comes to stand in front of me—hovers over me to be exact—and looks down.

"Were you a good girl?" he asks.

I nod my head and smile up at him as he reaches for my legs and lifts them to wrap around his waist while my back stays on the bench. I can feel him at my entrance.

"Tell me, does this pussy want my cock?"

I nod again, he's at my entrance now. Just about to slide in. And I try to pull him, just a little closer in with my legs where they are around him, but he has a hold of my hips and grips them hard.

"Be a good bunny and stay fucking still."

I bite my lip before he slides in, ever so slowly and fucking tortuous.

The feel of him filling me completely will be hard to compete with for any other man after this.

The feeling of how hot—how *sexy*—I feel right now as he stares down at me with so much need… that will be hard to replicate.

"Whiskey," I say his name as he slides in and out slower, only giving me the smallest grunt as he does so.

"Shut, up. Bunny. I want to listen to your sweet pussy as she milks me." He starts to move faster and harder. Fuck. Oh, my god. How am I meant to survive this.

He hasn't even finished fucking me yet, and I know I'm ruined for any other man. How am I meant to go on knowing sex can feel this good?

He fucks me so hard I have to reach for something.

"Hold on," he says as I look up and find the bars, gripping them on either side of my head for dear life. His fingers dig into my hips, and his body tenses with each push. I'm so lost in watching him, as the sweat beads down his chest and the look of pure lust that coats his eyes, I almost forget where we are.

I ride the wave of ecstasy. Thrust after thrust. He pushes me closer to the edge. Until I come. I come so hard I lose my breath. And I can feel him getting closer to his release.

He doesn't stop, and now my body is like a rag doll. His thrusts are causing the bench to knock into the equipment. I should probably be more aware of how easily those weights could fall on us, but I couldn't care less because it's already building and fucking exploding in me again.

Jesus fucking Christ.

He fucks like a god.

He comes, and as he does, he leans forward and grips my hair, lifting me up. His tongue, hot and needy, parts my lips, and his kiss promises one thing…

He is not done devouring me.

My hands find their way around his neck before he lifts me fully up while still inside of me. I pull back, breaking our kiss, and he just smirks.

"Who knew you were such a little whore?"

His words hurt. But then angers surges through me; how dare he call me a whore. He doesn't know a thing about me.

"Whore?" I drop my legs and pull away. His cock is still semi-hard and wet from my release. I can't get distracted by him…because fuck him. I'm no one's little whore.

"A good little whore," he adds, looking down and pulling the condom free. He must have noticed my disapproval of the little nickname he's given me.

"Fuck you," I spit out and spin away, but he reaches for me, his hot hands touch my body, turning me around to face him.

"You did that, sweetheart." He winks, and I pull my arm free from his grasp and reach for my clothes.

"Bunny."

I ignore him and start dressing.

"Is Bunny being a bad girl?"

"No, she is doing what a good whore does. Leaving."

"You're my favorite whore, Bunny!" he calls out after me with a small laugh as I walk out.

I see my shoes near the door, and I reach for them and don't look back. I go straight back to the party and thankfully see Emma talking to some dude. "I'm going home."

Emma looks at me, clearly confused, then she turns back to the bushes where I just came from and nods her head before waving bye to the guy and catching up to me.

"Shit, slow down and let me call an Uber."

I stop and slide on one boot followed by the next.

"You smell like sex," she comments.

I say nothing and she just smiles. "I'll get it out of you."

But she never does.

CHAPTER 4
WHISKEY
ONE YEAR LATER

There she is, in a red dress she should not be wearing to an event like this. It's her way of rebelling, of that, I am sure. Her father would have made her come—he always does. Somehow, some way, he has something over her.

Very soon, I will to. I watch as men walk up to them. Her mother stands proudly next to her father, holding his elbow, while my little Bunny stands there with a drink in her hand, her eyes looking dead to the world.

It's not how she usually dresses, in her loud and funky clothing. I see she's added to the ink that skates up her arm. I bet that made her daddy real mad considering his image consists of being squeaky clean.

She has no idea I am here. I stay back, watching her from afar. And I'd like to keep it that way for just a little longer at least.

"Sir." One of my men is trying to get my attention. I wave him off, and he steps back without another word. I can't be distracted right now. My attention is all on my little Bunny right now.

Her father keeps on mingling, while my Bunny gives them the necessary smile when needed. But that's it.

I never thought that when I saw her that day, standing outside in a leather skirt that I would become so fixated on her.

So entranced with her.

I've had my fair share of women. Fuck, I've even been married. And not once has any woman made me want to go fucking crazy like she has.

I've known her for so long, yet I feel as if I'm discovering something new about her every time I see her.

I heard she owns a bar downtown, the very same one she has worked at for the last few years. From my understanding, her father was not impressed. I've been keeping tabs on her. But I haven't approached; it's best I keep my distance and admire from afar.

That one could be dangerous, not for just me. But for my business as well.

She leans into her father and says something. Because I'm watching so closely, I notice how the man practically dismisses her. The way her father used to speak of her always baffled me—it was as if she was just *there*. Only to be seen, not heard. And I get the feeling that's how she is meant to be at events as well. He likes to show he is the good family man, but he's really just a crook with a lot of connections…

Aren't we all, though, really?

I continue to watch her from the bar as she pulls back and heads away from her family. She moves through the crowd, walking toward the restroom. I set my drink down and head in the direction she just went in. It's time, little Bunny, you've been away too long.

She slips into the ladies' room, and I wait at the door for a good minute before I slip in, checking there is no one else in here. I walk over and shut the door, locking it from the inside then lean against the sink as I wait for her to walk out. Her eyes are down when the door opens, and she automatically goes to the sink, but before she reaches it, her eyes lift and she spots me.

"Whiskey." Her breathing is suddenly labored,

and her eyes narrow. "Last I remember, you had a cock. So why are you in the ladies' room?" She pushes past me, unfazed, and starts to wash her hands.

"I missed you, Bunny." She rolls her eyes, it's slight, but I notice it.

"Could you not find another woman to be your little whore?" She scoffs. "I'm sure you can find someone at the party who would be more than willing to fill those shoes. I'm not interested."

"But you're my favorite whore. Why would I try to replace perfection?" I tell her. Oh, how I have dreamt of that fucking pussy. The way it felt, the way it tasted.

It was made for me.

I'm standing in front of the dryer as the tap turns off, and she eyes me.

"Move. I need to dry my hands." I make no motion to move, I just offer her a smirk. She smirks back at me and steps up closer to me, then places her wet hands on my shirt and starts to wipe them —all the while eye-fucking me with those enrapturing fucking eyes of hers.

Before I can even think, my hand shoots out and grips her arm, pulling her so she falls into me. My other hand grips her face as I slam my lips onto hers. Her mouth opens, and for the briefest of moments, I think she's going to give in to me. My torture ends as she kisses me back. Her tongue slide into mine, and her hands cling to my shirt, then she pulls back. I should know my Bunny isn't going to give in so easily.

She pulls away. I take the moment to really take her in. Her eyes meet mine, and I can't help but think how breathtakingly beautiful she is. From the curves of her hips, to the way her lips form into the shape of a heart—perfection.

Lottie Snow is nothing short of remarkable.

Pity she doesn't know it.

Her hands touch her perfect, pink lips, which are now swollen, and I've smudged her lipstick. She tries to wipe at it with her fingers, but all she does is make it worse.

Those green eyes are as crystal-clear as a perfectly flat lake, and they smash right into me.

"You can't do that."

"I did," I say smugly. And I'd do it again if she would stop backing away from me.

"I have to go."

"Do you?"

Her eyebrows pinch together in some sort of questioning movement. "Why do you do that?"

"Do what?" I ask her.

She shakes her head. "That! Just that!" She turns

back to the party happening behind the closed doors of the bathroom, and then, with one last look, she walks away from me as fast as she can before I can grab hold of her again.

I watch her go, smirking as her ass shimmies with each step before I decide its time I follow where the bunny wants to lead. It's what a good wolf would do, right?

As I come into the room, I notice she's already standing next to her father. My Bunny looks over her shoulder to where I am and spots me straight away. Her lips pucker, and I wonder what she's thinking when she stares at me. I can make a solid winning bet it's not the same thing I'm thinking. I smile a sinister smile, which makes her look away.

"I heard you were here. Couldn't believe it when I was told." Taking my eyes from her, I turn to see Clinton standing next to me.

"Clinton. Still hanging around the likes of the rich and famous, I see." The sarcasm dripping from my voice is more than evident by my tone.

"Oh, you know"—he puts a drink to his lips, looks around, then back to me—"trying to win myself a wife."

I say nothing and turn to look back to check on her. Bunny is now watching Clinton and I interacting with narrowed eyes.

"I almost had that one. Her father was keen for it as well." Turning my head slightly, I see Clinton looking her way, his eyes hungry as he watches her. "She called it off though, but man, I would like to fuck her again. All that ink with that red hair." He whistles and it's fucking annoying.

"She's about to become my wife, so I'd watch your mouth if I were you."

His eyes flick from her to me fast. "You wish."

"If you'll excuse me…" I step away and then stop. Turning back and keeping my voice low, I say, "You'll stay away from her, won't you, Clinton." It isn't a question.

"Yes." It's one word, but I don't believe it.

I'd be a fool to believe anything that comes from the filthy mouth of a man like Clinton. I open my phone, find the video I am after, and click *send*.

Her father wants to marry her off.

And I know the perfect way to help him.

CHAPTER 5
LOTTIE

One year.

One whole year since I have seen that man, but it's been almost every day since I thought of him.

Whore.

I am not a whore. In fact, I haven't been with a single person since him. "The nerve of him." I throw my bag on the floor. "You wouldn't believe it." I huff, reaching down to pull my heels off, my aching feet appreciative and waiting for some relief. Give me my flat shoes any day over these damn heels.

"Lottie…"

"Who does he think he is?" Pulling at the heel, I throw it, then reach for the next.

"Lottie…"

"He's just… so…" Pulling off the next, I throw it with more gusto than probably intended. Then I sit on the floor, cross my legs with my stupid full-length dress still on, and look up at Emma.

"What's the matter?" She stands in front of me, holding a piece of paper in her hand as she looks down on me. "Who are you talking about?" she asks.

"Whiskey. He was there tonight," I say, succumbing to the floor and lying down where I sit.

"Oh, my god. You're in a designer dress. Get it off that floor."

I stare at the ceiling, not even caring. Normally, I do care about my clothing, even the items I don't like to wear. But right now, I couldn't care less. Fuck the dress.

"He was just so…" I pause, opening my eyes to see Emma my best friend staring down at me, her face a mixture of puzzled and entertained. "So devilishly handsome. And he kissed me, it's still lingering on my lips—his stupid kiss."

Only it wasn't stupid, in fact, it was far from stupid. It was everything and more.

"What's his first name?" Emma asks. I stare at her blankly. *Is she not taking any of this in?* "Name, Lottie? Tell me his name."

"Whiskey." Her face drops, and she sits down

on the floor crossing her legs right next to me. "Emma, why do you look like that?"

She pushes the paper she was holding behind her back, then looks up to me with saddened eyes. "Tell me more."

"What's that?" I ask, sitting up, reaching for the papers behind her back. She pushes them farther back while shaking her head.

"Nothing. Tell me more about him."

"You're acting weird. Just show me."

"But you seem so happy yet pissed off all at the same time. I've never seen you this way about a man." I can hear the gush in her voice.

"No man has made me this angry." I reach behind her, but she pushes the papers farther away again. "Hey, let me have that."

She shakes her head. "No."

"Emma, let me see." Her phone dings, and she glances in that direction. So, I quickly reach over and take the papers from behind her back. Before she can pull them away, I'm up and walking with them to the kitchen.

"What's…" Whiskey's face is in the paper. Next to him stands a very beautiful brunette. "It says it's his wife," I read.

"Yeah, I think you just kissed a married man."

"I did not kiss him, he kissed me!" I scream. I

glance at the article and then look at his hand. "He doesn't wear a ring," I tell her.

"So, neither does your father," she points out.

"Shut up." I throw the paper and cover my eyes with my hands. "How could this happen to me."

"It was only a kiss, calm down." She waves me off. I scream into my hands. I cannot be kissing or doing anything with a married man. It goes against everything I stand for.

"Emma."

"Hmmm."

"I think I slept with a married man," I tell her.

"Sorry, what?" Emma's eyes go wide. "You had sex in the bathroom, not only is that unhygienic..."

"No Emma," I cut her off. "I slept with him a year ago, at that party." Pulling my hands away, I see her looking down at me.

"Why?"

"I don't know, it just happened." I shrug. "Am I a homewrecker?" I question her. I can't be a home-wrecker. Oh gosh, my father would kill me if he found out I not only called off my engagement, but then I slept with his friend. His very *married* friend.

"Calm down. I'm sure..."

I sit up when she goes quiet.

"What?"

"Okay, maybe you are a bit of a hoe. But come

on, he's hot, married or not, I'd ride that dick any day," she says, her tone serious. Seconds later, she's throwing her head back and laughs.

"This is serious," I tell her as my phone starts ringing. I reach it as a message comes through. It's an unknown number—one I don't recognize Opening the message, I see a video, and the minute it starts playing my heart sinks.

My phone falls, and I am afraid I won't be able to pick it up.

It's me and Whiskey. In his gym as he…

"Lottie, that's you," Emma says, coming up behind me looking at my phone.

His hands are in my hair, my legs are wrapped around his waist…

"Fuck, that's hot," Emma says.

"Asshole," I say, but I can't look away. It's like a train wreck happening right in front of my eyes. The hottest train wreck I've ever seen. One that I can't look away from.

I can feel his hands all over my body, as if I am right back in that night all over again. *How could I have been so stupid?*

"My father will disown me. This could ruin him," I say, who else has this, and who sent it to me?

"I'm more worried about you than him." Emma

comes up behind me, drops to the floor, and wraps her arms around my waist. She's right. Something like this getting out could absolutely ruin my reputation. "Call the number." I do, as she stays where she is.

"Bunny, I see you got my message."

No hello, no nothing.

"You presumed right, asshole."

"Oh, come on, Bunny. Is that any way to speak to your future husband?"

"My what?" I scoff at him, and I can feel Emma tense behind me.

"I didn't stutter, now…"

"You are already married." I stop him from going any further.

"*Was*. I was married."

"Were you married when we were together?"

"Tell me, would that upset you if I was?"

"Yes."

"Oh Bunny, do you want me."

I scoff at his words.

"In your dreams."

"I've dreamt of you, Bunny, have you dreamt of me?" Emma squeezes me from behind. "Bunny, one of my men should almost be there. Open the door for him." Just as he speaks a knock sounds. I hang up the phone and look back to Emma.

Another knock reverberates in the space as my phone rings.

"I'm not answering that," I tell her.

"That's okay, I will." She stands and brushes her hands down her shorts before she walks to the door and pulls it open. The knock comes again, and my phone keeps on ringing, but I leave it on the ground. Emma pulls open the door, and I see a glimpse of a man dressed in a suit.

"Lottie Snow."

"Sure," Emma says and holds out her hand.

"Are you Lottie Snow?" he asks again. He reaches for his phone, and I notice mine has stopped ringing. He answers it and then puts it on speaker.

"Bunny, I'd suggest you get up and take these forms." His voice rings through. "You won't like the consequences if you disobey."

"You aren't my father!" I yell out.

"No, but it seems you need to be spanked." Emma gasps and looks back to me, I can see the appreciation in her eyes at his words. "Take the paperwork, or my driver here will deliver it to your father instead."

"I wish I never saw you that night," I say, getting up off the floor. I take the paperwork the man is offering, step back, and shut the door in his face. Emma immediately takes it from my hands and starts opening it as I look on in shock.

"It's a contract," she states. "Hold on, there is more."

Sign on the dotted line…

I, Lottie Snow, agree to marry, Whiskey Corton, on the date supplied in the attached contract. In signing this document, I agree that I shall not, by any means, try to break this contract. I understand that if I do, the envelope held in escrow will be released to the parties identified within the contract, and I shall forfeit my right to the privacy currently afforded to me by the afore-mentioned Mr. Whiskey Corton.

. . .

I stand there, stunned. Not even bothering to continue reading it.

Nope. No way. This is not real.

"It goes on to say how he will release the video publicly as well as to your father if you don't agree to the arrangement."

"Well, I don't agree." I turn to see Emma, who's now standing with her arms crossed as she watches me.

"I don't want to say it, but I already know what you're going to do."

I stand and shake my head at her words. "You don't."

"I do because it's what you always do. You'll do what is best for your father. But think about this, Lottie. This is all about you. Your life. You need to do what's best for you. And marrying someone because of blackmail is not something you should do, no matter the consequences or how many orgasms he gave you."

"I never said I'd marry him," I tell her.

She walks past me and goes to her room. Opening the door, she looks back at me. "But you will. And my guess is that man knows this fact as well. How much did you tell him that night?"

"I don't remember. I was drinking." I cringe thinking back to that night. I told him a lot, that much I know for sure, but I never thought I'd see him again. *Fuck! How wrong was I?*

Emma's long nails tap on the door's edge. "I suggest you don't drink around him ever again. You know...when you're married." She smiles before she ducks into her room, shutting the door behind her.

CHAPTER 6
WHISKEY

I smile as I look at the screen of the camera located outside of my office. Her long, red hair is in waves and hanging down her back while she stares at my personal assistant. Today she's dressed as a pin-up model; it's a bit tamer than the look she was wearing on the night before at her father's gala. Her lips are pursed, and she's clearly angry because she's been kept waiting to see me for over an hour. Granted, I only found out about her presence ten minutes ago, but I like seeing this side of her. I love watching her anger. The way her plump lips push together in a thin line makes them even redder, and how she gets a slight wrinkle in her forehead indicating she's not happy. Angry Lottie is hot as fuck.

Her arms cross over her chest as she looks to the

elevator, which leads to the exit, and I can tell her patience is wearing thin.

I pull the door open, and her green eyes flick to me as her arms drop to her sides.

Quickly, and with no hesitation, she moves toward me until she's standing directly in front of me. "You," she seethes.

"Sir, I told her you were in a meeting."

I look over Lottie's shoulder to my personal assistant. "Thank you. Hold all my calls until Miss Snow leaves." I step back and hold the door open for Lottie to enter. She doesn't look at me when she walks in, her eyes trained straight ahead, but I take the perfect opportunity to stare at her ass in her tightly fitted skirt. Her red heels make her legs seem even longer.

"I can feel you staring at my ass. Stop it." She pulls the seat out opposite my desk and sits, not even looking back to confirm that I am, indeed, staring at her ass. I shut the door and walk around to my chair as she puts the contract on the desk. I smile thinking about that night—it wasn't what I expected. I'm glad she's nothing like I'd imagined in my head. She's better, so much more than perfect.

"It's a pleasure to see you."

"I'm sure the pleasure is all yours."

"Are we still angry, Bunny?" I ask, leaning forward.

"Angry? If that's what you want to call it. Sure, we can go with angry." Sarcasm is practically dripping from her tongue, and I can't help but smile. "Don't sit there and smile at me, Whiskey."

"But you're beautiful to smile at." It's true, she is the most stunningly beautiful woman, and she must know it.

"How could you do this? What can you possibly gain from this?" Lottie pushes the contract toward me. I look at it and notice it's not signed.

"You haven't signed it."

Lottie's head drops to the side. "Nope."

"And I take it you don't intend to?"

"Nope."

"Well, I didn't want to do this," I say while picking up the phone.

"Do what?" she asks as I call my driver.

"Yes. Please deliver the package to Mr. Snow. Be sure it's addressed as *urgent* from his daughter. Then please take the other package to the local news station."

Her face drops when I hang up the phone. "You're bluffing."

"Do you have your phone on you, Bunny?" She

nods her head. "I would keep that on you. My guess is your father will be calling soon."

"You wouldn't."

I lean forward. "Oh, but I did."

"How could you?" Her mouth drops open, and I want to kiss it. I want to taste her again.

"You had a choice."

"This isn't a choice. This is blackmail."

"If you want to call it that, but we could have had some fun along the way."

She stands with her phone in hand, then she looks up at me. "Father will hate me. You can't do this."

"Sign the contract." I push it toward her, and she looks at it with uncertainty. "It is only a year out of your life, Lottie. One year. Then I will destroy all evidence."

She blinks a few times then looks up at me again. "You shouldn't have the evidence anyway. How did you even plan this? You wouldn't have even known I was there."

"I'm a very resourceful man, Lottie."

Something crosses over her face, and then it's replaced with rage. Pure, unadulterated rage. She's furious. "Cancel delivery. Now." She looks at her phone, and I see her eyes glisten. "I never want to be a divorcee. All my life I have wanted to marry the one man who I knew I was going to spend my life with." A single tear falls down her cheek. "I wasn't even going to let my father choose that for me. I guess now, he wins, as do you." She leans down, signs on the dotted line, and then she stands, wiping her hands over her skirt before she turns to walk to the door. "You'll stop them before they reach him?"

"Yes."

She doesn't look back as she walks out.

And I almost feel guilty for what I'm about to do to her.

Almost.

"Stop staring at my ass!" she screams. And I can't help but smile.

Mine.

CHAPTER 7
LOTTIE

A glass sits in front of me, begging me to drink the contents. But I can't. Alcohol managed to get me into the dilemma I'm in right now. I can't stomach it getting me into anything else.

"Just tell me what's wrong with you. All you've done is mope and not touch your drink since you arrived."

"Father hasn't gotten any deliveries today?" I ask, looking toward his office.

"No, why would he? What's wrong?" My mother lifts a glass of champagne to her lips and takes a sip. Maybe I get my drinking from her.

I push the glass farther away. That needs to change right this minute.

I would like to say my mother was a nurturing

woman when I was growing up, but she was far from that. To her, I was a way to keep my father happy. He wanted kids, and she wanted him. And while she has tried, you can always tell its forced.

"I heard a story the other day…" I look up to see my mother already pouring herself a second glass. So, I continue, "One of the Governor's daughters made a sex tape, and her family disowned her…" I pause, giving her room to speak.

"Lucky for us, you aren't that stupid. Imagine what your father would do." She cackles.

I laugh. It is dry and false. All my life my father has had unrealistic expectations of me; it's something I have always known. He will gladly tell me when he is disappointed in me. It hurts to hear that often, so you do whatever you can to make them happy, while still rebelling.

"What do you think he would do?"

"Probably the same as the governor. Scandals shouldn't be present around us." She rolls her eyes and walks out, then straight back in with another bottle of champagne. "Why are you asking?" She pauses to think about my question, and then I swear I almost see a light bulb go off in her mind. "Don't tell me you did something stupid like this?" I watch as her hand starts to go white as she squeezes the bottle's neck, hard.

"No," I breathe through the lie.

Mom lets out a hard breath and goes back to pouring herself another glass of champagne. My father calls her name, and she walks off. When I check my phone, I see I have two messages. There's one from Emma, and I open it first.

Emma: You signed, didn't you?

She knows me well. I was hoping to prove her wrong. But as always, I do what's best for my family. Public image is everything to them.

Me: I'll explain when I get home.

The text back is instant.

Emma: I'll take that as a yes. I'll bring the chocolate.

Going to my other text message, I see *asshole* as the sender and wonder if I should even open it.

> Asshole: Engagement party will be in two weeks. Best to inform your parents now. Would you like me there when you do so?

What the actual fuck!

Two weeks.

Is he crazy? I didn't even think of actually telling my father I'm getting married. I guess I thought I could hide that fact from him. At least until I could make sense of this whole situation. Now, I'm guessing I won't be able to. But how do I explain the fact that I'm marrying my father's friend—which, come to think of it, are they even truly friends or just business acquaintances?

"Lottie, your mother said you stopped by." My father's presence is intimidating, always has been. I've never been able to lie to him.

He's always been an okay father, never around much unless it was time to show the family off by going to events. But...They have always been very vocal about the fact that I do not step out of line, that scandals are prohibited in this family, that they have no issue's with cutting anyone, even family, off—and they have, too. My mother's sister was cut off when she was caught dealing drugs, she was told to leave the city and never return. As far as I know, she could be dead. They never spoke of her again, but that's just one instance; my father has done that to many people. They come and go with his say. And despite how much I want to say or believe I am living my own life, I know that it would kill me inside to not have them there, even if they aren't the best of parents to me.

"Yep, I need to talk to you both."

My father scrunches his face up. "Can this wait? I'm waiting for a very important call."

I nod and he taps my shoulder as he walks past me to leave. No kiss or thanks for stopping by. I can't remember the last time my father gave me more than five minutes of his time.

"Goodbye, Mother," I say as I head toward the door, picking up my purse.

She stays at the office door, waiting to talk to my father. "Yes, see you soon." She doesn't even look my way when she speaks.

———

"He said what?" Emma asks, shaking her head. I show her the text message again. "So, does that mean you have to move out of here?"

"No. No way. You think?" *Oh gosh, I didn't even think of that.*

"I think you may have to. Otherwise, your father will wonder. And it's only a year, so just keep everything here and take what you need there. Then, when it's over, you can come back as if it never happened."

"A whole year," I moan. "That's so long." I lie back on my bed and press *call*, and it rings for exactly a minute before the asshole answers. "Will I have to live with you?" I ask, while squeezing my eyes shut.

"Yes."

I hang up the phone without saying another word.

A whole year of my life is gone.

"He said yes?"

I nod keeping my eyes closed. "He said yes."

"Okay, so we assumed this. Only a year, Lottie. Then, in the contract it says all evidence will be destroyed. You can do this."

I open my eyes. "Can I, though?" My phone rings and I put it to my ear. Whiskey has a set ring tone now, which isn't a particularly nice one; it says a lot of swear words.

"I'm at your door, here to answer all your questions. Let me in." I hang up the phone, sit up, and open my mouth, but I'm left speechless.

"Lottie?" Emma asks, getting off my bed, which I might add, is a mess due to me going through my closet to find the perfect outfit to wear to his damn office. Why I cared if I looked good is beyond me.

"He's here," I manage to say. Whiskey is here. At my apartment. And I'm not sure I'm ready to face him.

Here goes nothing.

"Shit! Really?" I can see the extra bounce in her step as she runs for the front door, and before I can stop her, the door is flung open, and Emma has her hand on her hip with her blonde pixie cut blowing strands in her face as she looks up to Whiskey, who's standing in my doorway. "You have some nerve, you piece of shit. Who the fuck does that? You need a fucking stick shoved up your ass so you know what it's like to be screwed by someone." Then, she steps back and slams the door in his face.

My eyes bulge from my head, and when Emma turns around, she's smiling. "That felt good. Okay, you can talk to him now." She walks off, smiling as she goes, leaving me standing there with Whiskey on the other side of the door. That is, if he hasn't left already.

Yeah, there's no way he's leaving. Whiskey is

the type of man to always get the last word in. This instance is no different.

Walking up to it, I pull it open with a shaky hand and see him still there. He looks me over as I yank the door open wider to let him in. Whiskey is dressed in a suit. Much like he was when I went to visit him when I signed the contract. He looked good then, but he looks even better now. Whiskey doesn't have his suit jacket on, just black slacks and a white button-down shirt. His sleeves are rolled up, showcasing forearms which are strong, tanned, and ones I remember very well from when they were wrapped around me.

"Your roommate seems—"

"I can hear you, asshole!" she yells, making me smile as I shut the front door.

"Interesting."

"Good choice of words, asshole!" she yells again.

Taking a deep breath in, I walk away from the door, leaving it open for him to enter as I pull out a seat at the table. Our apartment is pretty big, almost a loft-style. Our open-plan room with windows that are floor to ceiling, our two bedrooms are at the end of the apartment but before that is our kitchen and living room which you have to walk through to get to the bedrooms.

In between is a large rectangular wooden table with six white chairs surrounding it.

He sits at one end while I sit at the other, attempting to stay as far away from him as possible.

"What do you want to know?" His fingers tap on the table, and I glance at him—really look at him. He's always been very handsome. But now, the older I am, I appreciate the way he looks. Whiskey is a very attractive man. His chiseled jaw has considerately less stubble since last time I saw him. His strong, tanned arms are corded with veins. A watch sits on his wrist, and I know it's expensive because it's the same brand my father wears.

"When do I have to move in?" I ask. My hope is that I have time to get everything squared away in my life before I have to completely immerse myself in life as a married woman.

"When the marriage is official. But it may be better to do so before that so your parents don't get suspicious." His fingers tap again, those whiskey eyes locked on me.

"What do you get out of this?" His stare doesn't leave mine, and I feel like fidgeting in my seat.

"You," he states, staring at me.

"No, there has to be more than that. No one just

says they want to marry someone and records having sex with them. You had motive. So, tell me, what it is?"

"That I cannot do."

"Does it involve me?"

"No. You were just the bystander. A pleasant one, I might add."

"Do you do this often?" I ask, dropping my head to the side as I wait for him to answer.

"What, exactly?"

"Arrange marriages for yourself using blackmail?"

He chuckles at my words. "No. And I never intend to do it after you, either."

I cough and look away.

"You don't believe me?"

"No. Why should I? Because why do it in the first place? What's to stop you from doing this again to another poor woman?"

"You aren't poor, for one. And two, I have my reasons, and at the end of this, I will tell you."

"So, not before then?"

"No."

"Do you have any feelings for me at all?" My legs squeeze tighter as I wait for his answer.

"No. None. You are a means to an end."

"So, no sex?"

He smirks at that. "Not unless you beg for it."

That won't happen. Ever.

"Will you be sleeping with other people?"

"Possibly." My mouth opens at his words, but I say nothing. "Unless you beg, of course."

My forehead pinches together. "Is that meant to make me feel better? Do you really think I would beg you for something I have had."

"No." He smirks. "But I do recall you screaming my name."

"You must have misheard," I say in a voice that is high but fake.

"Would you like me to come with you when you tell your parents?" He reaches for something in his pocket and slides it toward me on the table. I look to the familiar blue box.

"What is this?" I ask, even though I already know the answer. "Do I really have to wear a ring as well?"

"Yes, it has to be believable. This will make it believable." Reaching for it, I open the lid. It's beautiful. Simple. And everything I would have picked for myself, should I have had the opportunity. "If you don't like it, we can exchange it."

"It's fine. It'll do." I close the box with a click and leave it on the table.

"Is that all? Anything else you want to know?"

he asks while watching me. Whiskey doesn't move, he simply sits there waiting and watching me.

"No. Not right now, but I'm sure there will be more."

He pushes his chair out and stands, looking at me as he waits for me to walk him out. I don't want to. Actually, I have no intention of doing that, so I wave my hand toward the door, making him smirk. When I think he's about to leave, he turns and strides back until he's in front of me. His pointer finger reaches for my chin, lifting it until I am looking up at him.

"We could have fun with all this, you know. You don't have to hate me. It's nothing personal against you."

Fucking hell! Whatever! His words shock me. Nothing personal? Um, last time I looked it was me on that video and that's awfully personal, right?

"Its best you leave before I slap you across that arrogant face. Wouldn't want to fuck up that smirk, now would we?" I pull away from his touch.

"I like to be slapped, especially if it's by a pretty girl like you." He turns and walks to the front door. "You have my number, Bunny, call or message me. I'm free whenever you're ready to meet with your parents. I promise to be a perfect gentleman. After all, your father would expect nothing less of me."

He turns to open the front door. "I look forward to their excitement."

Then he leaves, and the door closes with a soft *click*.

There will be no excitement, I am sure of it.

My father will not be impressed at all with this news.

But I'm guessing the other news would hurt more than a stupid marriage.

Fuck Whiskey.

Literally.

CHAPTER 8
WHISKEY

"So, you're getting married?" Barry's sitting across from me with playing cards in his hands as he looks at me for a sign to see if I'm bluffing. I don't bluff—ever. I win. He knows this and is trying to rattle me.

"Yes." I give a simple answer while staring at my cards.

"And will I get to meet her soon?" Barry knows all the ins and outs of my life. He's seen me fall then get back up and do it all over again.

"Yes. But I'm letting her announce it to her family first." I smile.

"Oh, god. You really are going to fuck her over, aren't you?" Barry shakes his head and sighs heavily. He wasn't down for what I planned when I told him about it but knows why I'm doing it.

"No, I don't plan to, she is a means to an end."

"Okay, so… What should I wear to the engagement party?" he asks, but there's a definite smirk on his face. "Black? For…her…funeral?" He draws out the words and then laughs.

I look back at my cards as he lays his down. When I do the same, he swears. I laugh and pull all the money toward me.

"Fuck." Barry picks up his drink and downs it easily, then he waves the bartender over. "He's paying," he states while pointing to me, then he orders another round.

"I've given her almost a week, and she hasn't contacted me."

"You've been giving her time?" He laughs, knowing how impatient I am. "How's that going for you?" He shakes his head still laughing.

"I'm about to go over to her place after this."

"Should I come, you know, for backup? And to meet *my* future wife." He winks. "I mean, once she realizes what a catch, I am she's sure to jump ship."

"No. You can stay away from her."

Barry sleeps with anything that moves.

"Awww… Come on, man. You know she's going to love me."

I stand, throwing the money on the table to pay for his drinks. "You'll meet her at the engagement party, and it's best damn behavior, you get me? Her family should be there." He salutes me as I walk away.

I was married once, and technically I have only been divorced for a year now. Although, we separated over two years ago.

Serena was a hell fire; we were heated and wild for months. We got married young and stayed in the relationship even though neither of us were happy. Until Lottie. I knew that moment she invited herself into my house that night I would finalize the divorce. No other woman had sparked my interest like Lottie. We hadn't been living together for years, and it was just a matter of time before one of us gave each other the papers. It seems I was first.

I get into my car and drive, and it doesn't take long to reach Lottie's apartment. Stepping out of the car, I notice music—loud music. Then I hear her giggle. I remember that giggle well. This woman's like hot iron, she's branding me with the attraction, and now she's stuck deep under my skin like nothing I have felt before. I know better, though. I need to keep a level head if I plan to finish what I started.

Her and that leather skirt haunt my dreams.

Knocking on the door, I expect to see her friend

answer, but what I didn't expect was to see Lottie in nothing but a swimsuit and a large smile—until she sees me, that is. The smile drops, and her face turns to instant anger. Looking past her to the inside of the apartment, I see no one but her.

Lottie has her phone in hand, and she lifts it to her ear and speaks. "My future asshole husband is here. Have to go." She hangs up, letting the phone drop back to her side. "What do you want?"

"You haven't called." She shrugs. "Do you want me to come with you to tell your parents?" I ask, trying not to become angry at her complete and utter disrespect toward me. Though, I guess I'm not entitled to any respect, but nevertheless, it still makes me mad.

"You look pissed off, Whiskey. Why are you the one who's mad?" Lottie drops her hand to her hip, her very *naked* hip, and I try my hardest to not look down at her breasts. Those tits are so fucking perfect. I want to touch and lick every inch of her gorgeous, tattooed skin. *Fuck! I need to get laid.*

I crack my neck before I answer her, trying to avoid looking but failing miserably. My patience is wearing thin. "Next week is the engagement party." I look to her hand to see the ring is missing from her finger. "And you aren't wearing the ring."

She smiles. "No. No, I am not." Lottie turns and

walks away, so I get the perfect view of her fine ass. "I know you're staring at my ass again, Whiskey. You just can't help yourself, can you?" She flips her hair to the side when she looks back over her shoulder at me. Then she winks and disappears into a room. When she steps out, she has the box in hand.

"What's this for?" I take it from her.

"Drop down on one knee and propose to me, Whiskey. And mean it."

"You've got to be fucking kidding me," I say while shaking my head slowly.

"Nope! Still waiting." She taps her foot impatiently. "I see this as"—she drops her head to one side and smiles—"you want something, so why can't I get something out of it as well? Drop to your knee and propose to me. If I'm getting married, I want a story to tell." Lottie then shuts the door in my face, and it takes everything in me to not kick that fucking door back open. *Fuck! This woman is infuriating.*

Choices—there are three.

I could call her bluff and walk away.

I could smash the door open and demand she wear it right now.

Or I could do as she asks and drop to one knee and propose to her like she's asking.

I didn't really propose to my ex, it was more of a *let's get married*. What Lottie is asking for is something I've never done before.

I weigh all the options, which one would be better, and why.

For fuck's sake, her option seems to be the easiest and least painful of the three, though I have no idea how to propose. Dropping to one knee, I hold the ring box open and knock on the door. When she opens it, she's wearing a dress, but I can still see her bikini underneath it.

"Lottie Snow, will you do me the honor of marrying me?"

"Why do you want to marry me?" she asks, smiling.

I'm about to tell her why, when I push the words back down and tell her what she wants to hear. "I want you to make me happy, and in marrying you, it will make me very happy."

Lottie rolls her eyes. "I guess that's as good as I'll get it." She then flings her hand toward me. Taking the ring out of the box, I reach for her hand, taking it in mine and sliding the diamond on her finger. Once it's on, I look up at her to see her watching me intently.

"You should kiss me now."

I'm stunned by her words.

I didn't expect them.

"Joking." She laughs so hard she bends over. "I was joking." Then just like that, she rolls her eyes, steps back, and shuts the door in my face again.

CHAPTER 9
LOTTIE

Today's the day. The day I'm expected to tell my parents I'm marrying an asshole, and at that, one of my father's friends. A man who I've known—and had a crush on— since I was seventeen. The same man who is blackmailing me with a sex tape. I'm definitely leaving that last bit of information out.

They can't know that.

Even though I know if I did tell them, I could easily get out of this.

My father's reputation has to be squeaky clean, and a sex tape of his daughter, yeah, that would soil his standing in the community. And we can't have that. So, I have to go along with this.

Walking into Whiskey's office area, I'm met

with the same personal assistant. Her smile falters a little when she sees me, but she quickly recovers. "Mr. Whiskey is in a meeting."

"Tell him I'm here. Please… It's urgent."

She nods and heads off to inform him I'm here. I sit on the sofa provided, and within a few minutes, his office door opens, and he strides out dressed in a perfectly fitting blue suit.

Whiskey's eyes flick to the personal assistant before they fall back to me. "Urgent? What's urgent?" he asks, but I know he's also talking to his personal assistant.

"She told me it was, sir. You asked if Miss Snow came to the office to tell you straight away."

Whiskey nods but his eyes remain firmly in place on me. "Bunny, what's urgent?"

I stand, brushing my hands down the front of my skirt. My father usually prefers formal attire. He prides himself on having a daughter of elegance and class. But today I need all the brownie points I can get. So, I've dressed in a tight black pencil skirt, a light-pink silk cami, and I've finished the look off with a white jacket. A pair of Christian Louboutin sky-high heels? That's just the cherry on top. At least I'm not in a damn dress. Though, I would prefer to be dressed in the clothes I like—give me a swing skirt, flats, and a short cardigan any day.

"You'll be coming with me. Now. I have a meeting with my father in twenty minutes." I look at my small Tiffany watch, which sparkles under the light, then back to him.

His eyes flick to the ring on my finger, then his eyebrows scrunch together in a frown.

"You have to book a meeting to talk to your father?" he asks, clearly confused.

With a roll of my eyes I answer, "Yes. He's a busy man, you should know this."

Whiskey scratches his chin and looks back over his shoulder at his personal assistant, who has a blank look on her face, then back to me. "Give me a minute."

I sit as he walks off, and when he returns, he has his phone and keys in hand.

"You ready?" I ask.

He nods, and I follow him out.

———

He has a driver.

Actually, I'm glad he does. It might impress my father a little more, though I'm sure my father knows more about him then I do. My only winning card is knowing more about his penis and what he sounds like when he comes.

I hope so anyway.

We stay quiet most of the drive while Whiskey works on his phone, and I worry. I hope to god my father doesn't lose his shit at me about surprising him with an engagement and marriage.

Shit! Fuckity, fuck, fuck! My palms are sweating as we pull up, and I have to remember what I'm here for. My mind goes blank while needing to remember why I'm doing this and that it's for the right reasons.

"Just breathe," he says next to me.

Damn! I almost forgot he was there. Almost.

"Easy for you to say." I slide out, and the minute I do, he steps to my side. Whiskey touches my hip, and just before I can push him away and tell him to fuck off, he leans in close to whisper in my ear, "Probably best you don't do that. Especially since we are madly in love."

He's right, and I hate him for it.

Leaving his hand where he placed it, we walk up the stairs. As we get to the door, my mother opens it. Her usual perfectly fake smile is on display. She eyes Whiskey while she holds the door open. "This is a surprise. We weren't aware you were bringing a guest, Lottie; hello Whiskey."

I nod and it's all I can do right now because

every ounce of fight and sass—or whatever you want to call it—has completely left me in this moment.

"Pleased to see you again, Mrs. Snow," Whiskey says with a voice I don't recognize. He's super nice in a perfect gentleman way. I've never heard him use that voice before. *Asshole.*

"Yes, as you can tell, I'm very surprised to see you," she says, but it's laced with venom. Whiskey doesn't seem to care about her tone of voice.

"It's a pleasure to see you," is all he replies as he looks around. His hand stays firmly on my hip, and my mother's eyes narrow to it.

"What is this?" Her eyes flick to my hip then back to me.

"Is father free now?" I ask, trying to avoid the inevitable.

"I hope you aren't bringing him bad news, Lottie." Her eyes narrow on me, and Whiskey squeezes my side firmly.

"No. Is he free?" I ask again.

Mother starts to walk, and we follow her to his office. Father's sitting at his desk, his phone to his ear as he waves us in. When he looks up, his eyes drop to Whiskey, who's sitting close next to me.

Father says a few more words, then hangs up, but he doesn't bother to stand. "What is this,

Lottie?" His voice is stern and straight to the point. He uses that tone when he's not impressed with something I'm about to do or have already done.

"Mr. Snow…" Whiskey greets, and Father nods his head.

"Lottie?" Father questions with a harshness just like my mother's. They are obviously both suspicious, and the anger seething from both of them is becoming awkward.

Taking a deep breath, Whiskey squeezes my side letting me know he's there, which is a small comfort, I suppose. "I have an announcement…" My voice shakes, dammit! I try to remind myself that I need to begin this as someone who's not scared, but a woman in love.

What a laugh that is.

"I'm engaged," I spit it out like it's a bad taste in my mouth, and then I pull my hand free from behind my purse. I had it hiding the ring. "Surprise!"

My mother grabs my hand and looks at the ring to make sure it's real. "This is a joke, right?" she asks, her hand squeezing mine a little harder than I'm sure she intended, so I pull my hand free.

"No."

"You didn't seem that interested in him at the gala." My father poses the question more like a statement. I didn't even realize he saw us together.

This is go time. I need to make this lie believable. Make it sound legitimate. "I wasn't ready to tell you then."

"And you are now?" he asks. "You know who he is, right? What's changed?"

"This," I say, holding out my ring hand again, avoiding his other question.

"Is this what you really want?" my mother asks, almost in a whisper. "We can make *this* go away."

"I'm right here, Mrs. Snow," Whiskey finally speaks up.

"No, I don't want you to make it go away. This *is* what I want."

"We're planning the wedding already. The date's set, and it'll be in a few weeks. We hope to see you both attend."

I try not to roll my eyes at him interjecting and telling them that.

"No way! You can't marry someone that's associated with your father; he's a criminal!" my mother's voice screeches.

"I've been seeing him for a year now," I reply. Defending what? I don't even know.

"You were with Clinton." Oh yes, Clinton. The one they approved of.

"No. We met after Clinton."

"You think we should just buy into this? That for some reason you want to get married. You've clammed up every time I brought up marriage to you. And what? Now you want it? And this soon? You expect your mother and me to just accept this?"

He's blackmailing me! I want to scream it as loudly as I can, but I know it's useless. If I want my father's reputation saved, I have to suck this up.

"This is what I want. I simply wanted the power to choose the man of my dreams."

My father nods his head. "Well, at least you picked someone with a good head."

Ah-huh, now come the compliments.

My father's face changes, and I know instantly he's seeing the business side of this, instead of what it should be, a marriage of his daughter to a man who's not that good.

Father's cruel in that regard. I see it the minute Father realizes what it will do for his standing and career. Let's face it, there's never any regard for what might be best for me.

"What do you need from me?" my father asks,

then eyes Whiskey. "We will talk more about this wedding at a later date, congrats are in order." My father turns to my mother, and she hands him a glass of champagne. We all take one, but I make no move to drink mine.

Whiskey's hand drops from my side, his comfort, or what I thought was comfort, vanishes, and I almost feel the loss.

Almost.

———

Whiskey's quiet as he drives me back to my place. We left my parents' home after the celebratory drink and lunch. They all drank and ate while I sat there trying to work out if I'm having a nightmare or if this really is real.

It can't be real.

But for some reason, I can't seem to wake up.

"You aren't close with your parents, are you? I presumed you were."

"Well, *you* presumed wrong," I say, not even bothering to turn and look at him.

"So why do you care so much about their reputation?"

"Because he is my father, and reputation to him is everything, it means more than his own blood."

"Do you want to go to your apartment or see your new home?" he asks, changing the subject.

I have no idea if he lives still in the same place, nor do I care. I guess it would be smart to see, but right now I'm not in the mood. At all.

"Home," I say.

"You'll have to see it soon, Bunny."

"Not right now," I argue back.

The driver slows down, and I watch as my apartment comes into view. My hand is on the handle, ready to leave as soon as he pulls to the curb, and that's when I hear the click of the lock.

"Why are you in a rush, Bunny?"

"I just need to get out of this car."

"Away from me?" he asks.

"Yes, you are so devious," I say, not even bothering to lie.

"Bunny, maybe stop with the hurt rich girl act."

I swing my head around. "Hurt rich girl act?" I ask, the words sounding bitter as they leave my mouth.

"Yes. You were raised with money. You have money. Let's not pretend that you aren't a rich girl, rich girl."

"Fuck. You!" I basically spit at him as I unlock my door.

"You already did that, bunny, but if you want me to be your devious lover, I can, and you can be my devious beloved." He smiles as I slam the door and turn around.

Asshole.

CHAPTER 10
WHISKEY

Mr. Snow has called to make an appointment to see me the next morning, it's been a while since I have done business with Gerald but now it's all about to change. He's known to the community as the good guy, the loving family man. But we all know what a fucking lie that is.

I've been calling Lottie to organize this wedding, and I've got zero fucking response. No matter, I'll gladly ask my personal assistant to do it. She loves that shit.

Regardless of what Lottie does, how she reacts, or how she treats me, I have little care factor when it comes to her rich girl tantrums. It simply doesn't matter how much of a temper Lottie seems to have or how much she wants to deny the wedding. It *will* all go through, it *will* be perfect, and it *will* happen.

"You sent a suit to my house. It's happening then?" Barry steps into my office wearing an open shirt and black pants. He looks like he's ready to go out and get laid. Let's face it, he probably is.

"Yes. Wear it to the party this weekend."

Barry scratches his chin and shakes his head. "Who else is attending?"

"Business associates. Her family. You."

"Perfect show then. But will your fiancée be up to play?"

Just as I go to answer him, the door to my office springs open and in struts—yes, *struts*—my fiancée.

Dressed in all black with her hair tied up in a high bun, a corset wrapped around her tight little waist, and shorts so short I don't want her to bend over in front of Barry and give him a show.

I sit back in my chair as she walks over to me, not even giving a second glance to Barry. She throws a dress on my desk. "You think you can dress me?" Lottie looks down at what she's wearing then to the dress.

"Hello, Bunny, nice to see you," I say, looking up at a very angry face.

"Oh… it's Bunny today, is it?" She scoffs, staring down on me with fury evident in her eyes.

"No, rich girl Lottie."

She taps her foot on the floor.

"You have nicknames… already? How sweet," Barry says, causing Lottie's head to snap to him. Barry stands and holds out his hand. "I'm the better one of the two of us. The name's Barry, and you must be the way-too-good-looking fiancée of my dick of a friend here."

Lottie looks to his outstretched hand. At first, I think she won't take it, but she does, shaking it then offering him a small smile she never gave me. Which, in turn, makes me furious.

"Pleasure, I'm sure." She drops his hand then turns back to me.

"Take your *dress*," she spits. "And shove it where the sun doesn't shine." She spins on her heels and turns to leave.

That's when I stand. "The party is tomorrow, Lottie. You are expected to attend with me by your side."

Lottie turns around, her hand firmly on the door handle. "And I will do so, dressed in whatever I please. Definitely not with something you had your personal assistant pick out for me to wear."

She's more offended that I got my personal assistant to pick it out. *Well, that's interesting.*

"Actually, I did ring you, though you chose to not answer." My hands come down on the desk, hard, making a loud noise. I roll them into fists in an attempt to keep my anger at bay. Looking at her ring finger, I notice she's not wearing my ring. "And when exactly do you plan to wear the ring I gave you?"

"What does it matter if I do or don't? You get what you want out of this situation no matter what I do." Turning, she steps out, then slams the door shut behind her.

"Well, I *like* her," Barry says.

I completely forgot he was in the room.

"So did I."

"You've completely fucked that over now, haven't you?" Barry sits back, shaking his head with a smile that's way too large on his face. "You had to go and record yourself fucking her. Nasty. But I still want to know when I'll get to see that."

I swing my head around to him from looking at the door, thinking Lottie's going to come back in any moment, but I'm wrong.

"Never! That shit isn't for your eyes."

"But you're willing to make it public?"

I sit back down while shaking my head. "It was a necessity."

"Ah-huh! I bet she's good in bed."

I rub my hand through my hair. "Do you ever shut the fuck up?" I say, eyeing him.

"No. But do you ever tell me all the details? No, you don't. I tell you when I've had the best lay, and I fucking describe it. Fuck, if I recorded it, which I might do in the future, I will watch with you. Though, unlike you, I *will* get her approval first. We can have popcorn and watch me fuck her into the bed. Maybe it will teach you a thing or two about how to treat a lady."

"Fucking her into the bed?" I say, almost shocked by his words. When in reality, I shouldn't be.

"Yes, fuck her into the bed. Trust me, they love it when you go really deep."

"Okay, you need to leave. Don't you have your own business to run, instead of sitting here annoying me?" I open my computer and start it up.

Before he can answer, my personal assistant walks in. "Sir, Rock Vintage called. They asked that a purchase be charged to your card. Should I authorize it?"

"Who by?"

She cringes. "Lottie Snow."

I wave my hand at her. "Yes, yes, it's fine."

She gives a quick sigh of relief.

"Well, she works fast," Barry comments.

I press call, and Lottie answers this time.

"You didn't waste any time," I say, impressed.

"If you insist on dressing me, you might as well pay for it. You are dealing with a rich girl, after all." Then she hangs up.

I look to the phone—one thing I hate is being hung up on. And she likes to do things that annoy me.

"I like her even more. When you're done, can I have the tape so I can blackmail her into marrying me?" Barry asks as he stands. He holds up his hand at the look on my face. "Okay, okay, maybe I'll wait a month for your heart to heal, because she's going to destroy it. Of that, I'm sure."

"No, she won't, because she won't get access to it. Of that, I'm sure."

Pretty little rich bunnies play with you. Fuck you over for their benefit.

And that's exactly what Lottie Snow is, a pretty little rich bitch ready to break hearts.

Mine's not included.

CHAPTER 11
LOTTIE

"You aren't wearing that are you?" Emma says from behind me.

"It's rock vintage. It is classic." I stroke my hands down my pants.

"I'm pretty sure your father's expecting you to wear a dress."

"For once in my life, I don't care what he thinks about what I am wearing. The man's already getting what he wants—me marrying into power and money." I huff, putting in hoop earrings to finish my look. My hair is up in a high, curled ponytail, my top is sleeveless in black and white, and it hugs every curve around my breasts, while the pants accentuate my ass, and the corset sucks me in perfectly.

"Okay, well, are you at least going to wear that gorgeous ring?"

I look at it. It is gorgeous. It's exactly what I would have picked if I had a choice. Whiskey couldn't have known that though. And it makes me angry that, somehow, he managed to pick something I actually like.

Emma picks it up and walks with it over to me. "Put it on. You've committed to this for a year. Might as well start that year now. The quicker you do it, the sooner it will all be over with."

Sliding the ring on my finger, I look at it and hate myself that I love wearing it and like looking down seeing it on my finger. Especially when it wasn't by choice that it was put there.

"How are you with going into his house the first time?"

"I'm supposed to be there before everyone gets there. Whiskey says it'll help establish the pretense that we're a happy couple." I cringe, happy, yeah that's the opposite of what this arrangement is making me feel.

Emma looks at the clock, then back to me. "Let's go. Otherwise, you're going to be late."

With a heavy sigh, I go to my own engagement party. One that I didn't agree to. At a house that I am meant to move into. I'm not sure how much I like the idea of that.

————

His house is large, but I expected it to be so. It's probably not smart for me to have my first time here be immediately before our party, because I will have no idea where anything is located, but right now, I don't care. This was never meant to be a part of my life. I had a one-night stand that has literally fucked me over.

As we get out of the car, Whiskey's standing at the door waiting, and he's dressed to impress. And if I weren't so sour at him, and currently hating on him so badly, I would appreciate the way he looks a little more. Because he looks mighty fine. He's dressed in that black suede suit with an undershirt that's black as well. His whiskey-colored eyes stare at me and, somehow, hold me right where I'm standing. Emma nudges me to get walking, and I manage to put one foot in front of the other as I make my way over to him.

"You look beautiful."

"I know," is all I manage to say back.

Whiskey's lip twitches at my words. He smiles softly at Emma, who mutters an *asshole* under her breath, making me smile.

"Come inside. My house is now your house."

"Until the divorce," I say, watching his every move.

He doesn't reply, just opens the front door for me to walk in. "I see you aren't in a dress." His eyes travel my body from my designer shoes then over my designer outfit. "I prefer this." I see the hint of a smirk, it's not for him to like.

That grates on my every nerve, and just to spite him, now I wish I were in one of those designer evening gowns I despise so much, but not the one he chose for me, or better yet, the one his assistant chose.

"Luckily for me, I'm not here to impress… *you*."

The white-tiled floor clicks under my heels. I stop and look around. Every surface has a vase of white roses. There are servants holding silver trays of food—and champagne. As a waiter passes, he takes a flute, offering it to me. I shake my head, turning away from him. That's one thing I will never do again, drink around him. Obviously, that leads to serious mistakes.

"You remember Barry." Whiskey waves a hand to his friend as he walks in and stops in front of me.

Barry nods his head and turns to Emma behind me. "You brought me a treat, how sweet."

Emma steps forward, and I put my hand out to stop her. Reaching for her, I halt her steps but not her mouth as she unleashes. "I'd watch that tongue of yours, wouldn't want to lose it now, would we?" She winks and walks off.

Okay, so that wasn't as bad as I thought it might be.

Barry slams his hand over his heart. "How is it possible to fall in love this fast," he says, eyeing her ass as she walks off. There's no stopping him, he takes off after her, which makes Whiskey shake his head.

"How about I show you around," Whiskey says, breaking our silence.

All I can do is nod my head and follow him around. We walk past the kitchen, which has many chefs and servants in preparation for the evening, its large, so large that I wonder who even buys something that big if they aren't a chef to begin with, the white and grey theme with gold accents on the tapware is beautiful. Then we head up the stairs to a room and he opens the door slightly, all I see is a large bed, with grey covers and two side tables. "This room is mine." He quickly closes the door, not letting me look long before he heads to the room next to it. Opening this door wide, he lets me step inside. "This will be yours."

It's nothing special. There's a queen-size bed, a walk-in closet, which appears to be empty, and an adjoining bathroom. I stay just inside the door looking around then turn back to him. "And if I meet someone?"

His jaw tightens. "You are not to see anyone but me for one year."

I cross my arms over my chest. "And what about you?"

"I know how to keep things discreet."

"Okay, here's how it will go. If you sleep with someone, so will I."

Whiskey's mouth opens wide at my words. He's the only stranger I have ever slept with. What a mistake that turned out to be. Never before or after Whiskey, have I had a one-night stand, but he doesn't need to be told that. Every other man I've slept with, I have been in a relationship with.

"That's fair," he says surprising me, and for some reason I trust his words.

"You stay here, mostly?" I ask, looking back to his room.

"Yes. And my townhouse. Now, would you like to see where the party will be held?"

I'm taken aback by his words. When I walked into the foyer of this home, I presumed the party was going to be held there. It's more than large enough.

"No expense was spared. It's our engagement party, after all. It has to be believable. At least, for now." He starts to walk, and I reach for his arm. "What happens after? What happens when the year is up?"

"You get your life back." It's all he gives me, but he knows that's not what I was asking. "The guests will be arriving soon. Come along."

We quickly step down the stairs and through the house to two frosted glass doors. They are beautiful with etchings to let the light in. Stepping out, I'm at a loss for words. It's so stunning that I'm pretty sure it's taken my breath away.

It's a winter wonderland. There's a large marquee on the grassed area in the middle of gorgeous grounds. All around the marquee are large trees, each of them decorated with sparkling fairy lights, which dangle down from the branches. Stepping inside the marquee, there are large white trees filled with more fairy lights. The ceiling is also covered in glittering fairy lights and snowflakes hang down low. The walls are covered in lights as well. The tables are dressed in white, with a silver tree on each as the centerpiece to match the silver chairs. Snowflake decorations hang from the crystal glasses, giving it an even more magical feel.

"You like it?" he asks, standing beside me. I had almost forgotten he was there.

There's no point in lying to him about it. It's beautiful. Stunning. A lot of effort has gone into this, and it does make our case very believable.

"Holy fucking shit." I hear come from the other side of the tent. Emma steps into view, her eyes flitting around to every surface before she spots me with a way too close Barry right behind her. She smirks at me and turns away to keep looking. The room is stunning and hard to tear your eyes away from.

Barry follows behind her as she moves around. He's like a lost puppy dog.

"Maybe you should change," Emma calls out admiring the view. "Not that I don't appreciate your look, but it doesn't really gel." I scrunch my nose up at her words, knowing she's right.

Whiskey's hand touches my back, and I jump away from his touch as if it's poison. We all know it is.

"You can't do that. You can't move away from

me like that," he says through gritted teeth.

"Does it make you angry?" I ask him sarcastically. "Perhaps not as mad as being recorded without your knowledge?" I fire back at him.

"Touché. Now, I'm going to touch you. Our guests are arriving. We will greet them together." His hand comes to my back, and this time I only shiver at his lighter touch. It isn't strong when he touches me, but I can feel it's almost painful for him to do as well.

My parents are the first people I see arriving as we head toward the entrance of the marquee. They spot us, and my mother's eyes narrow to where Whiskey is holding me. I can tell straight away she doesn't believe it. She has a keen intuition, and she's not buying any of it. I don't blame her. If there's one thing I'm not, it's impulsive. I think everything through before I do it. I weigh all my options and come up with the best solution that's suited to me. It's a trait I got from my father.

"This is some party. How will the wedding top this?" my father asks, looking around. He's holding my mother the same way Whiskey's holding me.

"It was all Whiskey here," I say waving to him as his hand tightens on my waist.

"Well, you really stepped up, but that's to be

expected, you are a lot older and wiser." His words are meant to be a jab, but I ignore it.

As expected, my father's eyes check over my outfit, and I know he's internally cringing because I'm not wearing a dress. In his eyes, all women should wear dresses all the time. Pants are a definite no-no.

"Grab yourself a drink. I have more people I want Lottie to meet."

We start walking as my father nods, and I'm thankful he does that.

"I must admit, I didn't expect you to have such a strange relationship with your family," he says, then smiles as we step over to his next guest.

"You never asked." I smile as we stop in front of a man.

"Leonard, this is my beautiful fiancée, Lottie."

The man nods his head and looks to Whiskey with dark, broody eyes. "So, my sister not good enough?" Leonard looks to me. "No offense to you, lady."

I nod, turning to look at Whiskey, who has a tick in his jaw before he answers, "You know as well as I do that it was never going to work between myself and Serena, we divorced, and it was amicable."

"So, I see, maybe for you. You do seem to prefer

a *different* type." He nods to me again before he walks off with a huff.

"Your wife's brother?" I ask him, confused.

"Yes." He pauses. "It's no longer her I want. I've fallen in love with Lottie." His hand grips me harder, and I almost believe the absolute lies spewing from his mouth. Whiskey is after all a smooth talker, and I feel like he could tell you the sky is pink instead of blue and somehow you would believe him. His eyes pinch when they look at me.

"Why did you end it?" I ask just above a whisper.

"Because of you. Now, let's move on, shall we?" He turns, stepping back into my space, touching my back.

"Did you love her?" I ask.

Whiskey looks at me. "Maybe a little," is all he gives me before someone else walks over to shake his hand, and his drops his from my back. I pay no attention, thinking whatever it is he wants from me must be important if he's left a woman who he could have loved, for what he seems to think he can get from me.

Whiskey goes to touch my back again, and I pull away. "Lottie," he chastises me.

"What?" I bite back. "How many people know?"

"Barry. No one else."

I smile, but it is fake.

The party must go on.

CHAPTER 12
WHISKEY

Lottie's good, I'll give her that much. She hides her anger and unleashes it when it's just us. My hand stays on the small of her back as we make our way around, even though I know she doesn't want it there. I don't have many people here I know personally. I like to keep my circle small, mainly so I don't get fucked over. It's usually the ones with the most money that stab you in the back the fastest.

Let's hope my Bunny isn't the same.

"We should sit."

She nods. The food is coming around, we've been mingling with the guests now for a good thirty minutes while everyone arrives, and apart from her questions earlier it's been ok.

"How much longer?" she asks. I pull her seat

out, she smiles, and I realize she's been trained this way. Lottie has been trained to be the perfect lady at events. Turning to look at her father, I see him watching her closely. Does he instruct how she's meant to act out in public as well? Her father sees me staring and nods his head before he turns to his wife sitting next to him.

"At least another hour, then they will be gone."

She crinkles her nose, not liking that answer as the food is placed in front of us.

"A toast," Barry yells, sitting next to me.

Lottie's eyes flick to him in worry, but I place a reassuring hand on her leg, which she stops bouncing then pushes me off.

"I've never seen Corton so in love. I'm glad someone as beautiful as Lottie has managed to tie him down." Barry winks at Lottie, her cheeks reddening, and it makes me remember that night where I made them blush bright red. When I fucked her and told her all the dirty things I wanted to do to her.

"To you both. I wish you nothing but the best."

I raise my glass, and so does Lottie.

Everyone cheers before we look out and see her father standing.

"Lottie, I love you. You are one of my greatest achievements." I turn to look to her and notice she's smiling, but it's forced. You can only tell if you look closely enough, and I've gotten to see this reaction often. "I'm happy you found a man who's brave enough to tame you and handle you, because you need it, maybe the age difference will help." He chuckles, making everyone else but myself and Lottie do the same. He goes quiet, raising his glass while staring at me. "Treat her well, Whiskey. She's yours now. Welcome to the family." He sits back down, and I turn to Lottie. Her hand touches the glass of champagne in front of her, but she doesn't lift it. It's as if her hand is frozen.

Leaning in close, I say, "You can drink it, you know."

Lottie's eyes, which are full of fire, turn to me. "And let you take advantage of me again? No, thank you, very much." Her hand reaches for the water as everyone starts eating. She doesn't touch her food.

"Do you plan to make this difficult?" I ask, leaning in close so no one else can hear.

She turns into me, her mouth coming close to my ear so no one can see or hear what she's about to say. "I hate you. Hate you. This isn't my thing. This is just one more thing a man is making me do. Fuck you!" When she pulls away Lottie smiles elegantly. She waves to the waiter to take her food and reaches for the dessert plate instead. I watch as she eats a slice of Bavarian Black Forest gâteau, then she proceeds to take mine too.

"Hey, asshole." Leaning over, Emma's looking my way. She's sitting right next to Lottie who's too transfixed on her gâteau, so she doesn't pay either of us attention. "Think you can call this shit display off anytime soon? I want to go home, and I need Lottie with me."

"She's staying here tonight."

The fork Lottie has in her hand pauses at her mouth.

"Actually, a mover will arrive tomorrow to collect all her possessions. You'll be in this house for a year starting from today."

Lottie's fork drops heavily onto her plate, and she looks to me, that perfect smile in place not showing how mad she is, while everyone looks up at the noise. They all go back to what they were doing quickly after she says, "Sorry." Then she turns to me and whispers, "We're starting this tonight? I don't get one last night in my own home? I should have figured you take that last shred of happiness from me."

I don't answer her. Instead, I stand.

"Thank you all for coming. I would like to announce here to you all tonight before you leave, please stop by the cake table to grab your invitation to the wedding. It will be held in two weeks." Then I sit back down.

"You... c-can't."

"I just did."

————

Guests stay and mingle a little longer than necessary. Lottie stays rooted to her chair the entire evening. Seated next to me looking at her champagne but never touching it.

She thinks I would do something again while she was drunk. I didn't actually fully plan our last one, but she hasn't asked either what I do for work.

When she knows I think she will work it out.

Plus, I don't think she really paid much attention that night to things around us, just us.

That night will forever haunt me, not only because it was fucking perfect. But I have a feeling no other woman would ever compete.

"Guests are leaving, your parents look ready to come over." She straightens at that, and instead of watching them I watch her. Her hair throughout the night has fallen down. Or she pulled it out, either way it looks beautiful. I can smell the faint vanilla; it must be the shampoo she uses.

"Two weeks, that was a surprise," her father says. "Whiskey, it's been so long since we have actually spoken business, I think we should soon. What do you say?"

"Yes, I will get my assistant to ring yours." Her father's eyes fall to Lottie's; her green eyes match his.

"Goodnight, let me know how much you need, and I will pay."

"I plan to cover the wedding," I remind him. "As you stated, Lottie's now my responsibility. I'm fortunate enough to be able to take on these costs. I just ask that you join us and enjoy yourselves."

"It's what the father of the bride does," her mother chimes in.

"Yes. But we've got this, thank you." Lottie stands, leans over the table, and kisses her mother's cheek. Her ass in perfect view again. She kisses her father, and I can't help but look. She has a great ass. When she pulls back, she leans in close as they walk off.

"Stop staring at my ass." I can't help but smile as a few others say goodbye, when it's just us she turns in her seat to look at me. "You disgust me." Her hand lifts and she slides her hair from her head. I lean in real close to my perfect fiancée and whisper in her ear. "Was it so disgusting when your lips were wrapped around my cock." I pull back, and she gasps at my words. I can only laugh as she gets up.

And watch as she attempts to leave.

My bunny, oh how I plan to play with you.

CHAPTER 13
LOTTIE

I wake in a strange bed. My heart starts beating erratically not knowing where I am. Then I remember where and why I am here, so I let out a loud sigh. Climbing out of the bed, I reach for my clothes and slide them back on. I slept naked, as I have no clothes here, though I don't sleep with clothes on anyway, so it was no big deal. I head to the kitchen to find Whiskey standing there, dressed and ready for his day with an earpiece in his ear as he talks incessantly. I stop, waiting for him to turn around to acknowledge I'm here. He spots me but doesn't say a word. Biting my lip, I contemplate going back to my room, but it's the weekend, and the weekend is my time. I don't have any events that, as the daughter to the senator, I must attend and usually I'd go to the beach and spend the day there doing absolutely nothing but reading a good book. It's the perfect day.

"Do you have plans?" He startles me when he finally speaks, and I look up to him.

"Yes," I lie.

He senses it's a lie straight away. "Your things will arrive in twenty minutes. I suggest you wait for them." Then he walks off. Once he's gone, I head to the fridge to see what's available. My usual breakfast is in there. I turn to look for him to ask him how he knew, but he's long since gone. How on earth does he know what I eat for breakfast? Coconut yogurt, strawberries, and peanut butter. I know it's weird, but once you try it—heavenly. Taking all three ingredients out, I make my breakfast and check my cell phone. My father has tried calling several times, and if he doesn't hear from me soon, I'm afraid that outcome probably won't be great. But I also wonder now if he would do the same old guilt trip he would normally do now Whiskey is in the picture.

"You're too busy now for your own father?" he answers. Clearly, he's not impressed by the sound of his voice.

"I was sleeping. I've just woken. It was a big night last night."

"Indeed, it was. I can't say I wasn't surprised.

But it was a pleasant surprise. You will be marrying well. I'm pleased that you will be taking care of your family." I should have known my father would make this about the family. Who cares if I'm happy or not, right? He's fishing for truths and lies, but luckily, I know all his tricks.

"Whiskey and I feel its best." I say, almost choking on the blatant lies I'm spewing. Am I trying to convince him or myself more?"

"Good. Good. You'll be marrying well then."

I cough. If only he knew. But would he really care, considering I am marrying Whiskey? A man who Father can gain traction from being associated with? Yeah, I doubt it very much.

"Yes," I manage to squeak out.

"We want to pay for the wedding. It's tradition." My eyes bulge at that statement. I scoop another spoonful of my breakfast, ignoring him as he continues, "I'm sure you can convince him. Tell him, no budget."

"Sure."

"Lottie."

"Yes, Father."

"Divorce is not an option, you hear me?" Why is he bringing divorce up? Shit, does he suspect that this is all a ploy? "You stay, no matter what.

Marriage is a life commitment." My spoon freezes. "Lottie," he says when I don't answer.

"That's not up to you, father."

"So, you're keeping it as an option?" Dad's fishing, the asshole.

"No, but that's out of your hands. I would never stay married to someone I don't love."

"So, you aren't sure if you love him?"

I place the phone down and mute it, then I scream, loudly. I can hear him saying my name when I unmute it.

"I love him." Shit! That tasted like acid when I spoke it, a caustic taste that burns my mouth.

"Good, as long as you're sure. Hate for the newspapers to write about how my daughter marries then divorces straight away. They will think you've done it just for the money." There's no point in me speaking anymore. He's digging for more information that I don't want to give him.

"Okay, I'll be off then. Send the accounts for your wedding straight to your mother. She'll handle it all." Then he hangs up with no goodbye. And so, I repeat the process, screaming at the top of my lungs. One day he will hear me. One day he will know how frustrated he makes me. Maybe.

"You really have issues with your father, don't you?"

I freeze, then slowly turn around. Whiskey's leaning against the door, his hands in his pockets as he watches me.

"How long have you been standing there?"

"Long enough to hear you admitting just much you love me." He gives me a smug look while bringing his hands to his heart, looking like a teen girl who's talking about her first love. "I also heard the scream. But I'm not sure if it was frustration or just because you can't contain your feelings."

That bastard. He's enjoying this too much.

"Fuck off," I say, turning back to my breakfast.

"Such a filthy mouth. Wonder what Daddy would say if he heard how much of a dirty girl you are," he throws back at me.

"He doesn't, and it will stay that way." Turning back to him I ask, "How did you know what I eat for breakfast?"

Whiskey straightens his hands and they come out of his pockets. "I take notice of things that are important to me. You're one of them." Then he walks off, leaving me at the kitchen counter, angry at the two men in my life.

One is meant to love me no matter what.

The other is using me for his own personal gain.

And right now, I have no idea what that even is.

———

"Just run away and never come back," Emma says as I walk into my now empty room. Everything was packed up and delivered to my new house, one I never signed up for, one I would never have picked myself.

"That means they all win. How can I let them win when that's all they ever do?"

"You give them that choice, you know that, right? You know how to use the word 'no,' but when it comes to your father it's a non-existent word in your mind."

She's so right. I know this. But it's easier said than done. If I disobeyed him, I could ruin his career as well, and his career is what paid for my schooling and helped me become who I am today. I don't have it in me to do that to him, even though I know he manipulates me into being something I'm not.

Even in my best attempts at rebelling against him I still somehow listen to everything he has to say.

And then we have Whiskey, what's his real motive.

"I just don't know his angle, and I really want to know why."

"Well, it's not your money. Clearly, Whiskey's richer than you."

"That he is." His house and his lifestyle prove that.

Emma puts on her hat as we start to leave. "Beach day?" she asks, smiling while reaching for a bottle of wine to take with us.

"Yes, please." Pulling open the door, Barry stands there, his hands in his pockets and a playful smile written all over his face.

"Oh, fuck, no! You go away, right now." Emma shoos him, but he simply finds her amusing.

He looks to me. "Can you see the love, it's so evident in her eyes."

I reach for the bottle of wine from Emma's hand before she throws it at him.

"Whiskey asks that you call him. Said he's been trying to reach you all day." Then he turns to Emma. "You and I have a date."

"No, we don't." She slams the door in his face.

I wait for her to calm down as she walks back and forth, back and forth, until she stops and faces me after wearing a line in the carpet.

"I don't like him. I hate that you're in this position, and I wish I could remove you from it." Emma's hat that was originally on her head is now in her hands. She straightens up, puts it back on, reaches for the wine, and grabs the door handle. "Go! Go to his office, annoy him as much as you can today. I'm going to do some digging." Then she opens the door to Barry, who's still standing there. He smiles upon seeing her as she steps through the door, hooks her hand through his arm, and off they go.

———

Whiskey's office is quiet. It's the weekend, but his light is on, and I can hear him talking on the phone. Pushing the door open, I don't even bother knocking as I barge in. He looks up from his computer and continues his conversation but stares at me. It's business, but the way he speaks makes me think he's talking directly to me.

I step over to the wall where a photograph of a man is hanging. He looks like Whiskey, except older.

"That's my father. This was his business."

"And what exactly is this business." I cross my hands over my chest as I wait for him to answer.

"You didn't google it?" he asks.

"Emma did, but the only conclusion she could come up with is that you're rich."

"You are rich," he adds.

"True, so what makes you rich?"

"Bad men," he says, and a shiver goes up my spine.

"How?"

I notice the phone is down on his desk, and he's watching me, and not answering me.

"Are you close?" I ask, stepping away and over to his desk. My fingers run along the hard wood until they come to the corner.

"We were. He's dead."

"I'm sorry."

Whiskey shrugs and closes something on his computer before he looks back up to me.

"You didn't answer my calls. Again."

"I was busy."

"So, I heard." He stands from his desk, and now that he does, he's closer to me, only inches away. He leans in, so we are even closer, and I can smell his cologne. It's a masculine scent mixed with something sweet. I like it. A lot.

"Your father called, asked what he needed to pay for."

"Did he?" is all I manage to say back breathlessly.

"He did. I don't want money from your father."

"It's not for you, it is for our wedding. It's what a father does," I argue back.

His lip lifts and he shakes his head. "No. I will be paying for it all. I won't be taking one dime from that man."

I heard his accent, it got thicker when he's mad. I've never noticed it before.

"Why are you staring at me like that?" he asks, but just before I can tell him, the door opens, and heels click on his floor. I turn my head at the same time he does, and when I do, I see her. Blonde hair as white as the clouds in the sky. A dress—I try to not laugh, but I'm not all that successful—that's so short I can almost see the color of her panties. And eyes so blue you'd think you were staring at a deep ocean.

Her eyes flick from myself to Whiskey, then they stick on him. "He told me, but I didn't believe it." Her eyes fall to my hand where *that* ring sits, and I have the urge to move it around to hide it away from her eyes, because it's as if I'm physically hurting her. "So, it's true. You are engaged?"

"Serena," Whiskey says, but I already realized it's her, I've seen pictures, but she looks different her hair is shorter and the pictures I see she's always dressed in some type of gown. The way Whiskey says her name, it's laced with feeling and emotion. It's the first time I've seen or heard anything like it from him. Serena's hands clutch her sides, and tears threaten to break free, but somehow, she manages to hold them back.

"I loved you. I would have given you all of me," she says, as if I'm not standing between the two of them, is she choosing to ignore that I'm the one currently wearing his ring on my finger?

"I know," he replies, "but we agreed, you knew we weren't right."

A single tear leaks free from her eye and runs down her cheek.

Whiskey moves from next to me and strides toward her. All of a sudden, I feel as if I'm the interloper in this room. It's funny because I am, and I know it. His hands touch her face, and he wipes away the tear with his thumb. Serena's eyes stare right into Whiskey's, I'm even starting to wonder how he can walk away from that. From her. Clearly, she loves him. And he obviously feels something for her too. Otherwise, he wouldn't be holding her like she might break.

"Why, Corton? Why?" She says it with such pain laced in her tone. It's interesting that she's calling him by his last name.

I exhale, loudly. She seems to remember I'm here and looks back at me.

"Lottie, it's time you leave."

Whiskey pulls her face back to his, and she looks to him with hope.

I don't argue, she can have him.

I have no *care* factor when it comes to Whiskey.

Even if it hurts just a little to walk out that door.

CHAPTER 14
WHISKEY

"Who is she?" Serena asks the minute the door closes behind Lottie, and I drop my hands from her face.

"I met her after you."

"And what, you love her?"

"No," I answer truthfully.

She looks at me confused. "That makes no sense, Corton. You either love her or me. Why pick her?" she asks.

"You can't win this one, Serena. It's Lottie I need to marry." I don't want to argue with her, but I know this is what she wants.

"No, it's not. We can get on a plane to Vegas and get married again. It's obvious she doesn't even love you. I could see that by the way she looks at you. She practically ran out the door when you asked her to leave. All the while you stood in front of another woman. She doesn't care. I do. I want you."

I try not to smirk at the thought of Lottie wanting me to kiss her. I want to do exactly that, bite those fucking lips and claim her damn mouth. The urge is getting stronger each time she shows me her fiery sass.

"You should go." I turn to walk back to the desk.

"Marry me, Corton. Please." Her hands touch me, and she's immediately pulling at my belt. Serena's hand quickly goes down my pants until she has my cock in her hand. She strokes it and leans up close, so her lips are at my ear. I can't deny, her hands feel amazing wrapped around my cock. "I know you love it when I wrap my lips around your cock. Let me take care of you, baby. I'll make you remember why you married me in the first place." Serena bites my ear, as I reach for her hand between us and pull it from my pants, my eyes travel up, and when they do, I notice Lottie is at the door looking in through the glass with a look of absolute disgust written all over her face. She turns and walks off.

"You should go, and don't come back, Serena. I

don't love you." I seethe, "And if you ever come in here again and do that shit when I am married, I will make you regret it, I gave you enough money to last you a lifetime. Leave. Now."

"She isn't even blonde!" she screams and walks out. I once had a thing for blondes, now it seems fiery red heads are more my type.

———————

"You get your dick sucked by your ex often?" Her voice startles me, she's sitting in my personal assistant's seat. *How long has she been here?* It's been hours since Serena left.

"Where have you been?" I ask.

"Around." She's spinning in the seat like a child would. Now is not the time for games nor her sass. I walk over and stop her mid spin. She looks up to me with an abundance of hate and with her eyes narrowed in on me, the fire in her eyes make me want to lean in and extinguish it with my mouth. "Not sucking dick… that's for sure."

"You should have left."

"So you can have your dick sucked in private?" she asks, her eyes not even blinking.

"No, I don't mind an audience," I answer her back, making her stand.

She pushes her hand against my chest in anger, and my cock instantly hardens at her touch.

"No. We already know that since you like to record it. Tell me, do you do that to all the woman you fuck?"

Reaching for her hair, I push her back, but she shakes her head away from my touch.

"That privilege is reserved only for you."

"Aren't you a fucking sweetheart." She pouts her lips at me.

I go to bite at her lips, but she pulls away before I can make contact. Too bad it's not far enough to keep me away. "I can be yours, sweetheart, if you want to wrap those naughty lips around my cock." I thrust my hips, and she looks at me in disgust.

"That's never happening again." She doesn't move when she says it.

"Are you so sure?" I argue back. Her face goes red, and her temper's now flaring.

"Positive. It was a mistake the first time. One I'm not willing to make again." I can see the defiance, but I can also see the want.

"Are you sure about that? Can you look me in the eye and say I wasn't the best fuck you've ever had?"

"You most certainly were not." I smirk at her words.

"Lies," I say back to her.

"I was actually thinking of going out now to get laid. Since we discussed this and I now know you're doing that, I might as well and we aren't married yet." Her eyebrows bounce up and down at the tease.

"No, you won't. You will not be going anywhere to fuck anyone."

"Try to stop me, you asshole." She pushes against me to move, but I don't. All she does in the process is rub her sweet little body all over mine, making me want her even more.

She notices a minute too late, and before I can stop myself, I reach for her hair, pulling it and bringing her face closer to mine. My lips touch hers, and I remember exactly how she tastes. Fucking sweet. Sweet as the most delicious cherry.

Her lips don't move at first, until I press my body into hers a little harder. Then she gives in, her mouth opens, and I take full advantage. My tongue slides into hers, and just as I pull our bodies closer, she does the unthinkable.

She fucking bites my tongue until I taste the metallic tang of blood.

Pulling back, she smiles. There's a touch of blood on the side of her mouth.

"You think you can have what doesn't belong to you just because you have money?" she asks. Lottie steps away from me as I wipe my mouth.

"You bit me."

"I did. And I won't hesitate to do the same if you try that shit again." She quickly walks to the elevators, and I do nothing to stop her.

"I'm going to make you beg, Bunny. And I'm going to fucking enjoy it."

"Hey, Whiskey…" She flips me off, keeping it in the air as the elevator doors open. "Sit on this and rotate, asshole." Then she walks into the elevator with a smile so evil, if I didn't know better, I'd say I will need to watch out for her.

Lucky for me, a red stop light has never stopped me, so why should a red-haired vixen do the same.

CHAPTER 15
LOTTIE

The fucking nerve of him. Honestly, how dare he? Who does he think he is? Kissing me as if he has my permission to do so. My anger has reached an all-new level of boiling point. Driving back to where I now live, much to my disgust, I walk directly into the house and beeline it straight for his bedroom. Pushing the door open, I notice the bed is made and everything's in order. If he thinks he can treat me any way he pleases, he's wrong.

I'm not his puppet.

And I'm definitely not his Bunny.

Walking over to his surround sound system, I play the last song he listened to. I turn it as loud as it can go before I kick off my heels and walk over to his closet. Opening it, I see all his perfect suits hanging one by one, side by side. The amount of money hanging here is ridiculous, Armani, Gucci, who even needs this much money hanging from their closet? I start pulling every drawer open. Then I empty the contents onto the floor, dropping each one as I go. A pair of scissors drop to the floor, and I pick them up. Oh, I have an idea. If he thinks he can fuck with me, it's only lady like that I return the favor. Stepping back to his closet, I start tearing up each and every one of his perfectly lined up suits until they fall to pieces on the floor. Then I reach for everything that's high, pulling that down so as to make a complete and utter mess of his perfect little piece of solitude.

He deserves this.

No, he deserves more.

Plus, everything is replaceable to him.

He has the money to buy whatever he likes.

"What the fuck are you doing?"

I turn to find him in the doorway, the look of anger is evident on his face. Good. Welcome to how I feel, asshole.

Turning away from him, I continue to pull down his shit because I don't give a shit. "Redecorating," I reply with my back to him. "It's what a good wife would do."

Hands wrap around my waist, and they lift.

"Put me down." I slap at his hands as he throws me onto the bed, and I bounce. It's the only place where I haven't made a complete mess. I start laughing, and soon he's standing right next to me.

"You're fucking crazy! You know that, right?" His eyes pin me. "You just destroyed thousands of dollars' worth of my things." He climbs on the bed, and my laughter stops instantly as his body hovers over me, and those whiskey-colored eyes lock onto mine. "Do you want attention, Bunny? Is that why you're doing this?"

Looking up at him, my eyes narrow. "Get off."

"You came into my bedroom first Bunny. I didn't come to you."

"I can smell her on you."

Whiskey licks his lips. "My tongue is sore, and yet, I still want to kiss you. Do I take the risk?" he teases, leaning in close. His lips pause at mine. "Or, perhaps I could destroy your things as well." He pushes off me, but as he does, I feel his desire for me. It was evident as well when he kissed me, but then it made me mad thinking of watching him with her. Whiskey reaches for the scissors and starts heading toward my room. It takes only a second to click as to what he's said, and I jump from the bed to see him already in my room, tearing at my things.

I reach for him, but he shrugs me off.

"Oh, my god. That's vintage. Put that down," I scream at him.

"These?" He holds them up, and with a snip of the scissors I used to ruin all of his things, he's now doing the same to me. Before I can think of what I'm doing, I am jumping on his back. That doesn't stop him, though. He continues grabbing my stuff, paying me no mind. I reach for his hair, pulling at it, trying to make him stop. He drops the scissors and steps back until my back hits the wall. I drop my legs from around him, catching myself before I land on my ass. He turns fast, so fast that his body is now pushed against mine. Every inch of him, every inch that I don't want, is now on me.

"Get off," I manage to speak.

"You don't want that, now do you?" He pushes me, and my body rises to meet his. I hate myself for it, but my body wants what my mind doesn't.

"Get. Off," I say through gritted teeth all the while somehow leaning in.

"Harder did you say?" Whiskey pushes closer, and I have to stop myself from grinding on him. It's very fucking hard, considering I know what he can give me. To know what he is packing and how he can make me feel.

I don't have to start grinding because he does. All the while, his eyes never leave mine.

"You're pushing your limits," I say, becoming breathless. My eyes close, and I push back into him. It's been too long.

"Tell me you want it," he whispers near my ear. "I can smell you. I know you do."

"I want it." Dammit! The words betray me. My body betrays me.

"Beg for it."

My eyes fly open at his words. "Beg?" I manage to speak.

"Yes, Bunny, beg."

My hands push on his chest. "Get off of me, you scum. There's no damn way I am begging."

"We'll get you there. You will beg." He places a chaste kiss on my forehead and pushes back, getting off me. "Clean up your mess and stay out of my room."

The asshole walks out, leaving me in my room all hot and bothered.

————

I don't come out of my room until the next day,

and I only come out when I know he's left. I watch as his car drives away, and when I walk into the kitchen, my breakfast is made and sitting on the counter with a note.

You can't avoid me forever.

Are you kidding! I sure as shit can try.

————

It only lasts one day before he comes into my room uninvited. I'm getting ready for work, and he stands there like he always does. Half in and half out, eyeing me with those eyes. Pulling my skirt up, I slide the zipper up and turn to face him. I only have a bra on—a red lacy one—that any sane man would be drooling over. Every man except Whiskey. And I'm a little disappointed.

"What do you need, Whiskey?"

"You."

My face whitens at his words, and I have to turn around so he can't see the reaction he makes me have. "And pray tell... why do you need me, Whiskey?"

"Because my ex is here. With your parents. So, get dressed and make her believe you love me." His words stun me, so I quickly pull on my silk shirt, tucking it into my skirt, before I slide on my heels and walk over to him.

"You owe me new clothes."

Whiskey leans in close. "You owe me a whole new wardrobe. I had to send for things from my apartment," he replies, clearly not happy.

And just that fact alone makes me smile.

"Let's play happy," I say, clapping my hands. Standing in front of him, I lean in close, so our lips almost touch. "Games are my favorite thing." I wink at him as we walk out.

Whiskey stays behind me, and I can feel his eyes on my ass as we walk into his living room. His hand comes to the small of my back, and when it does, I see Serena standing at the door with her purse clutched in her hands as my father sits on one of the sofas.

Standing, my father looks to me then to Serena. "I wasn't aware you had company," he says as his eyes come back to me. "And Corton's ex-wife as well," he states, looking to Whiskey.

I reach for Whiskey's hand, pulling it from my

back and lacing my fingers with his. "Neither was I."

Serena looks at our hands, her eyes narrowing. "You want her?" she spits from across the room, but her eyes never leave ours.

"It's best you leave, Serena." Whiskey's voice is firm.

She folds her arms over her chest. "I don't think I will." Her hip pops out to the side in defiance.

My father looks back to us, our hands glued together. "I have security out front," he says, offering them to us.

Looking to Serena, her eyes go wide.

Whiskey steps toward her, dropping my hand.

I pull him back, so he stands next to me. "Yes, please, escort her out of *my* home."

"Your home?" She scoffs. "I was fucking him in this house only a year ago?" she screams. "Does she have her own room, too, Corton? Or is she the lucky one?"

My father's bodyguard walks in and makes his way to where Serena is standing. Her hands fly up in the air. "I can escort myself out. I just came to tell you that our dog died."

Well, damn. You can hear the sound of a pin drop. What the fuck, I didn't even know they had a dog.

Serena walks past us, and no one moves. His hand squeezes mine hard, almost to the point of breaking, and I have to pull my hand free from his grasp.

"I'll be back," he says, following where she's just left, and I watch him go knowing he's going to speak to her.

"You should go and stop that before he leaves you for her. Don't want to have to send a cancelation out," my father says, sitting back down. And with a wave of his hand, he instructs me to go after my fiancé.

I do. I was going to anyway.

"To think you could move on so easily," she says at the front door.

I stop, waiting to hear what he has to say.

"Why wouldn't you have told me earlier?"

"It worked, though, right? Got you to come talk to me," she says sweetly.

When he speaks next, I can tell that he's angry. Seething, actually. "Is he even fucking dead Serena, what the actual fuck." She shakes her head no at his words. Which in turn makes him even madder. "To use that. To say that. It just proves you aren't meant for me."

I step around the corner, then walk over to him, sliding my hand in his in front of her.

"Leave, you aren't wanted here," I inform her.

Her eyes fall to my hand in his and she straightens. When she looks back to him, I can tell she is hurt. "You were meant to love me. We had something. You know that you've made me this way. I'm not this type of woman, Corton. It's unfair. Especially, now that you have moved on so fast." Her fists close up, and she shakes her head, her eyes beginning to water before she turns and walks out the front door.

The minute she's gone our hands don't separate, we just stand there not sure what to say or do. My father is in the other room, so words need to be carefully spoken.

"You didn't have to get involved," he finally says, turning to face me.

Our hands stay joined, and when those words leave his mouth, I try to pull my hand away, but he doesn't let it go.

"And look like a fiancée who doesn't care? No, thanks." This time I pull harder to get my hand free and his grip loosens. Before I can walk away, though, his hand comes out and catches my waist before I can get any farther away. Pulling me back to his front, so now he's behind me but our bodies are touching, he leans down and whispers in my ear, "We could make this arrangement fun for both of us. Care to add a sex clause into the contract?"

My back straightens at his words.

How dare he?

"Why? Your booty call just leave? So now you need to add a new one?" I question. Then I laugh, pulling free as I walk toward where I know my father is waiting. I stop, turn, and lift my dress so he has a clear view of my ass. "This booty isn't for your calling." Then I drop my dress as he bites his lip, and I walk away from him.

CHAPTER 16
WHISKEY

She has on a fluorescent pink G-string and an ass that I want to bite. Badly. I didn't think she had it in her to be feisty and a tease all in one go, but she does. Walking back into the living room her dress now down covering that ass, she's sitting with her legs crossed and her dress no longer showing that extraordinary ass. Walking over close to her, I sit on the double sofa and drop my hand on her bare thigh, I feel her tighten under it, as I look up to her father. Lottie's father doesn't miss the touch, he just nods his head.

"To what do we owe this visit?" Lottie asks. "A surprise one too," she murmurs, sounding surprised herself.

"Not that you're not welcome, Gerald." I use his first name. "But is there a reason for your visit?"

"Yes." He looks from me to his daughter. "Someone has whispered to your mother that this is all fake. I want the truth. I don't need anything blowing back on our good family name."

Fucking hell, he really is a dick.

It makes me smile knowing what a fucking asshole he is, and what he deserves.

"Who said that?" Her hand covers mine and she squeezes just before he answers with, "Clinton."

Lottie's hand leaves mine and she stands.

Her father's eyes follow her. "Sit down, Lottie. I told her his lie won't help, so this is why I'm here, to inform you of what's happening."

"I told you he wasn't right for me. But you didn't believe me," she says, her eyebrows rising.

"Sit down, Lottie," her father orders her.

"I'd watch how you talk to my future wife like that when I'm around. You may be used to talking down to her, but I won't have it." I feel her eyes on me, her mouth opens, but she says nothing as she looks back to her father.

"No, I have to get to work." She walks off, leaving me sitting in the same room as her father, a man I don't particularly like, to say the least, but I've also known him a lot longer than I have known Lottie.

"I hope you understand what you're in for when it comes to her." He shakes his head.

"I do." I don't, but he doesn't need to know that.

"I knew your father. Did you know that?" he says, surprising me.

"I did." I think he forgets how we met.

Gerald's eyes open wider, like he wasn't expecting me to say the truth. "Tragic what happened to him. How that all played out."

"Yes. Yes, it is," I say, agreeing. "Now, is there anything else you need, Gerald?"

"I take it she told you I will be paying for this wedding, it's the least I can do. Hopefully, my daughter only gets married once."

"She did mention it. There's no need, I have it covered."

Gerald stands, Lottie walks back out with her bag slung over her shoulder, ready to leave.

"You are planning on taking me to work, aren't you?" she asks me. Lottie looks to her father. "Next time you feel the need to stop by, call first." She offers me her hand, and I get up and take it. Her father starts to walk out, and soon it's just us standing there. Lottie drops my hand like it's burned her the minute the door is shut behind Gerald.

"What happened to your parents?" she asks. I should have known sooner or later she'd ask. "And how did my father know them?"

"My mother died over twenty years ago. My father died when I reached eighteen. It was my birthday present to find him hanging from our garage ceiling."

"Oh, my god." She gasps loudly. "I'm so sorry. So, so, very sorry." She goes to reach for me.

"It happened a long time ago," I tell her glancing at her hands that pause before they touch me, I want them to touch me.

"I'm torn between hugging you right now and still hating you," she says truthfully.

"Why can't you do both?"

Lottie shakes her head. "I need to get to work."

"Let me drive you."

Her hand goes to her hip. "What do you mean? I was expecting you to." Then she walks out straight to where my car is located and opens the passenger door.

I follow closely behind her, and then we head off to the bar.

She hardly talks on the drive over, simply works from her phone until we get closer. "I'll be finished early, pick me up around seven?" Then she goes to get out.

"No goodbye kiss?" I ask her.

"You know what you can kiss, but I'm not showing it to you again." She smiles sweetly as I stare at her ass.

I would like to kiss that ass. Bite it. Take it. You name it.

That's one fine ass.

———

"How long do you think you can play this game for?" Barry asks as we sit at the bar. He asked to meet me for drinks. And I had time to kill while I wait for my fiancée to be finished with work.

And I had to go to a bar that isn't hers. I'm already stealing so much of her life; I have to be careful what I take.

I've never had to chaperone a woman, let alone pick her up and drop her off to work before. This is all very strange and new to me.

"Till the contract is done. Then I'll let it play out as it will."

He rubs his hand over his jaw. "And you don't care if you hurt her?" he asks me.

"She's tougher than I thought. She'll be fine."

"Will you, though?" he asks. "You said you

thought you loved Serena, and now what? You just…moved on?"

When I think of Serena, she is automatically removed and inserted is the picture of a red head, with dazzling green eyes.

Serena was a change, and maybe if I'd tried hard enough, I could have stayed in love with her. Maybe. But I'm not, and there's no changing that.

"Moving on."

"You don't have to. You could make this real. Try with Lottie. You might find you like her more than just a bed mate."

"Don't go getting all sentimental on me now, Barry, just because you have goo-goo eyes for her friend." He smiles, not even trying to deny it.

"What I don't get, is why you waited so long?" he asks. "You took the video a year ago. What made you not use it then and go back to Serena?"

"I liked her and felt bad." I shrug. "But then I realized, in the game of business all cards must be dealt. I have to deal mine to get what I want, and let's face it. Feeling bad for a woman, is low, even for me."

"I just hope you know what you're doing, and you don't fall too hard for her, because if she finds out why you really wanted her to sign that contract, she will hate you and there's no turning back from that."

"She will find out...in a year. Until then..."

I drink what's left of my glass and leave.

It's time to pick up my fiancée.

CHAPTER 17
LOTTIE

Whiskey's waiting when I finish. I didn't expect him to be, but I'm a little relieved when I see him. I turn around to find him leaning against his car, his suit jacket undone and just a touch of chest showing.

"That man could bounce a quarter off that chest," Bianca whispers next to me.

"Bianca, this is Whiskey." Whiskey's eyes flash to me when I say his name. "My fiancé." Then I feel Bianca's eyes on me. I work with her every day, and I haven't told her I was dating anyone, let alone engaged.

"You're engaged?" she asks, shocked.

"Yep," is all I can manage in reply.

"To him?" she asks, pointing.

"To me. It's a pleasure to meet you." Whiskey

offers her his hand.

"I mean, I can see why you'd want to strap that down. But wow, Lottie. That's fast." Whiskey watches me as I cringe.

"I'll see you tomorrow." I wave to her, and she just walks off.

"You work together?"

"Yes, for quite some time. I made her manager because she's really good at what she does."

Whiskey opens the car door, letting me in. "Do you want her at the wedding?" he asks. Leaning down to look at me, his gaze captures mine, and it takes so much to look away from him. I'm exhausted, and the last thing I want to do is play games with Whiskey. Clearly, he wins them, the sneaky bastard.

"I'm not planning it, so I'm not sure who is invited," I tell him.

"I know. I already have it planned. Luckily for you." He shuts the door. "Do you want to go out? Make this real?"

"None of this is real, Whiskey. This is just a trumped-up fantasy of yours. For god knows what and why. I have a life, and I don't want to play a part in yours." I'm tired and fed up with his bullshit.

Whiskey takes off quickly, the wheels skidding

out and his hands squeezing the steering wheel so tight they turn white. "I've been trying, you know, to make this smooth. To make this not be so bad for you. But you make it real fucking hard, Bunny."

His words shock me.

"Me? Make it hard? Oh, I'm sorry. Didn't realize it was you getting blackmailed and forced to marry someone you don't love and only fucked once." My voice is full of sarcasm.

"And I've tried to make it easier, tried to make it so when it's over, we won't have any ties. But you're making it very fucking hard."

"Fuck you."

"You say that a lot to me. Is that perhaps something you want to be doing? Fucking me?"

"No. I've made that mistake already," I retort.

He slams on the brakes, his hand coming out to stop me from jolting too far forward. Then he turns in his seat. "You're a real fucking bitch right now," he says, as a horn honks behind us. He doesn't move.

I lean in closer. "Yes. Yes, I am." I pause. "I'm the one you fucked, remember," I say, my head dropping to the side.

"What a mistake that was," he replies.

"I couldn't agree more, asshole."

A horn honks again, and he takes off, not saying

another word until we reach the house.

He starts quickly speaking as I step out of the car. "By the way, you're in my bed tonight. I've burned yours."

Then he walks inside, leaving me standing next to the car looking at his retreating form.

What the hell?

————

There isn't a bed in my room anymore, it's now empty. Not even my clothes are in here. After taking off my heels, I carry them in my hands as I walk to the door next to mine, to his room. He's sitting on the end of his bed, paperwork in hand, and when I turn to look at his closet it's full of clothes, and not just his, mine as well.

"We aren't sharing a bed."

He looks up. "Feel free to sleep on the floor then, but I must say my mattress is heaven." Whiskey stands, removing his shirt as he walks away and into the bathroom. I watch as he goes. Once he's out of sight, I look for pajamas, which is going to be hard, considering I don't sleep in any. Finding an old shirt, I place my heels in his closet where all my other things are located.

I decide to head to my old room for a shower. When I reach the door, I find it locked. *Ugh.* I walk back to his room, and he steps out with a towel wrapped around his waist. My heart picks up speed, and I have to remember to look away.

I stare at him.

I want him.

That's evident.

But only someone ridiculously stupid would want someone who's using them. And I don't want to be used.

"Do you need help getting undressed?" His words seem to unfreeze me.

"My bathroom is locked," I manage to say.

"Yes. I told you this is your room now. That room is being torn apart." He walks to his closet and drops the towel to the floor. His ass comes into view and words seem to evade me. I watch as he doesn't bother dressing just turns around.

All I see is cock.

A lot of cock.

I cover my eyes and hear him laugh.

"If I remember correctly, you weren't covering your eyes last time," he says as I peek through my fingers.

"Yes, but in my defense I was drunk."

"Is this why you won't drink around me now?

Afraid what you really want will come through?" Whiskey teases as he comes closer in all his glorious nakedness.

He pries my hands from my face until I have to look at him. When I do, my eyes focus everywhere but him—a very naked Whiskey.

"You can look. Hell, you can even"—he leans in closer—"touch."

My eyes fling wide open. "No!" Then I walk to the bathroom, my body brushing against his as I pass. The minute I get into the bathroom, I shut the door, lock it, and lean back against it.

One more week and we will be married.

How am I going to deal with him for an entire year?

I'm fucked.

After showering and coming out, I notice he's already in bed with a book in his hand.

"You read." I walk around to the other side of the bed and reach for the pillows, making a border down the middle of the bed—one he's not allowed to cross.

Whiskey stops reading and looks at me. "Sleeping with me requires a fort?" he asks, some-what amused.

"Yes. Sleeping with you isn't something I want to do," I say as I climb into bed, pulling the quilt up over me, then turning over, so my back is facing him.

"Goodnight, Bunny."

I close my eyes, and believe it or not, I have the best damn sleep I've had in a long time. Despite sleeping with a blackmailer right beside me, one who also happens to have a marvelous body and terrific dick.

Asshole.

———

"Rise and shine, sleeping beauty." I wake to Emma standing next to my bed, actually not my bed. Whiskey's bed. Her arms are crossed over her chest as she looks down on the bed I'm still trying to sleep in. I turn quickly to see Whiskey's already gone and breathe a sigh of relief. "He let me in. Said your snoring woke him up." She cackles.

"I don't snore."

She rolls her eyes at my words. "Please, and I'm the fairy godmother of dicks."

"You could be," I say, thinking about a great dick I was dreaming of. Gosh, I hope I didn't talk in my sleep.

I get out of bed, and Emma looks me over. "What? No naked sleeping?"

As she says it, Whiskey walks in with a coffee in hand. "You sleep naked?" he asks, with an eyebrow raised.

"Wouldn't you like to know?" I take the coffee out of his hand and stand in front of him while he's dressed and ready like he's been up and waiting for hours.

"I do," he says.

Emma takes an intake of breath, making him smirk even more.

"Emma's here with you to go wedding dress shopping. The store has my contact info already on hand. Buy a dress for each of you." He reaches into his suit jacket and passes me a card—a black card.

"I don't need this. I earn good money." He shakes his head.

"Use it for whatever you buy for this wedding, I don't want you to be paying for it."

"No." I push the card back at him.

He pushes it straight back to me while taking a step closer, his breathing harder, and I have to remember I don't like this man. "Take the damn card, Lottie." He places it in my hand, then walks out of the room.

"That's hot," Emma says.

"What's hot?" I ask, not looking her way.

The card in my hand burns. Is he buying me? This feels all kinds of wrong. I toss the card on his side of the bed and start getting changed.

"You like him, don't you?" she asks.

Lifting my eyes from the skirt I'm sliding on, my gaze narrows.

"Don't look at me like that. You like him, but you're fighting it. This is going to be an interesting year. Maybe I should start taking bets on how long you'll last."

"Last?" I ask, not really wanting to know what she's going to say.

"How long until you fall hard for him? Or at the very least, sleep with him. Whichever comes first."

"I did just sleep with him," I say, smiling.

"Haha, smartass. You know that's not what I'm talking about."

"I met his ex. I think he could still love her," I say in a whisper.

"What?" Emma stands off the bed.

"We look nothing alike. Why is he doing this if I'm not his type?" I look to the door to make sure he isn't lurking there because he has a habit of doing that.

"Clearly you *are* his type, or he wouldn't be making you sleep in his bed," she replies.

"She loves him, and somehow, I feel bad for her," I say with a shake of my head.

Emma gives me the loudest sigh. "Please, you didn't send yourself a damn blackmail contract. He wanted you. Which, by the way, you need to start finding out why. Don't be naïve in this. He *is* using you. And if you want to, use him too. You can, Lottie. Fuck his brains out and make him love you."

"Oh, yeah, because sex makes you fall in love."

"I think you can make him love you." I shake my head at her words. "Think about it. He's doing this to you. You should do that to him. Make the man love you."

Her words are not something I've thought about.

Maybe I should make him love me.

Payback can be a bitch.

"He'd know, wouldn't he?"

She shakes her head. "He doesn't have to know a thing. Just be yourself. Pull away, only to be pulled in. Hook, line, and sinker." She winks.

"He said I'd have to beg if I wanted him," I tell her, and it makes her eyebrows raise.

"Well, my love. Start begging."

CHAPTER 18
WHISKEY

Lottie doesn't move when she sleeps, she sleeps like the dead. But damn can that woman snore. How could something so beautiful make a noise that loud. I go before she wakes. What's the point of staying?

Her father is waiting at my office when I arrive. Gerald's been showing up a lot lately when he hasn't been invited, which is surprising since Lottie had to book to see him last time.

He wants something.

What, I don't know, yet.

He smiles when he sees me, and I lift my sunglasses from my head when I see him, offering him my hand. When I shake it, I realize it feels as fake as he is.

"I don't want to involve my daughter in business, and since you're about to be my son-in-law, I thought why not speak directly to you." Gerald puts a hand on my shoulder and taps it. "You can make time for your future father-in-law, can't you?" he says, and I only offer him a nod as we take the elevator to my office.

"I take it you don't want me speaking to Lottie of this visit?" I ask as the elevator door closes slowly.

"No need to. I came to visit you, not her."

Of course he has. The snake.

The elevator comes to a stop, and we both get out. My personal assistant looks at me, then back to her work. I learned early on not to play with people I work with, it cost me thousands of dollars when I first started out trying to fix a mistake.

Pulling out my phone, I send her a message. Just because I may be using her, does not mean I like it when others do so. And her father has used her enough.

Your father's in my office. He told me you didn't need to know.

"What can I help you with?" I ask as I sit.

He cracks his neck from side to side. "I came to

see if you wanted to invest in a charity I'm operating."

"Invest?" I ask him.

"Sponsorship. We are always on the lookout for people who are willing to help sponsor and make this city a better place. You have the means to do so, so I figured what better person to ask than my future son in law." When he stops talking, he looks around the office.

"Your father created something very special here. I'm glad to see it didn't die with him."

My company runs and owns chains all over America. We sell everything from fridge's, cars, to phones to guns and everything in between, but my main income, is security. Anything you need, we have. And it almost died, well, it practically did die, just before I took over. One of our CEO's was running it into the ground, and there were only three stores left open. When my father had it, we had over a hundred stores open and doing remarkably well. Now I have it, I've tripled the business since I added security, I have a thing for watching people. So, yes, I have the money for whatever it is this man wants, but he's silly if he thinks he can play me.

I help some of the most dangerous men in this city, once upon a time, I helped this scum bag.

"Me too." He nods. "If you send me all the paperwork, I'll be sure to look through it and let you know if I can sponsor, but as you know, I have my own charities as well."

"Oh, yes, suicide. Well, I know that one is close to the heart, but you should do more." I do, but he doesn't need to know where my money goes. That's none of his fucking business.

Gerald's phone starts ringing, and he holds up a finger as he goes to answer it. "Hello, Lottie." I sit back waiting to hear what he has to say. "No, I can't meet now, I'm in a meeting. Let your mother know when she knows my schedule." Then he hangs up, and my phone immediately beeps.

Lottie: Is he still there?

I reply straight away.

Me: Yes.

"You sure you know who you're marrying?" he asks, joking as he stands from his chair.

"Do you know her?" I ask, making him pause.

"Lottie has a rebellious streak, so watch her closely. She's trainable if you do it right."

"Thanks for that advice. Though, I don't want to tame her," I say, standing with him.

"Are you sure about that?" he asks, as if he can't believe what I've said.

"Yes, I like her just the way she is."

"Only *like*." He taps his phone. "I see."

Fuck! I've fucked that one up, didn't I?

"I like the way she is. I love her as a person."

A simple nod to my lie is all I get in return as he turns and walks off. When he gets to the door, he stops before he pulls it open. "You know, privately investing in a charity is good for publicity. Our other sponsors have great connections as well. International, too."

"I'll keep that in mind," I tell him as he walks out.

My phone starts ringing and her name flashes across the screen. *Bunny.*

"He just left."

"What did he want?" she asks, not even caring to say hello.

"Wants me to become a sponsor for one of his charities."

"Of course he does, because then that makes

him look good." I can practically feel the eye roll I know she's giving.

"What do you want me to do?" I ask her, sitting back in my chair, waiting for her to respond.

"You want my opinion?" she asks, sounding almost shocked.

"Yes, Bunny, tell me. You *will* be my wife soon, or have you forgotten?"

"That's a hard thing to forget when your ring sits on my finger every day," she says with more sass than she started the conversation off with.

"That's not answering my question. Do you want me to give your father money?"

She doesn't speak straight away. I can hear her breathing on the phone, though. "No."

"Okay then, I will decline his offer."

"Whiskey."

"Yes, Bunny."

"You're using me, aren't you?"

I could deny it, but it wouldn't be the smart thing to do. "Yes."

"At least you didn't lie about it. Now I don't feel so bad for buying the most expensive dress there was in the designer store."

Lottie hangs up, and I can't help the smile that sits on my face.

CHAPTER 19
LOTTIE

I didn't lie to Whiskey; I did buy the most expensive dress. Though, I didn't know that until the lady rang it up behind the counter. The dress is a designer's dream. It's the exact style I would choose for my real wedding. But since I won't be having one of those—at least not any time soon—I'm choosing to make this as realistic as possible. Just that the ceremony will be missing that *in love* part.

"Whiskey," I say when I answer the phone.

"That dress is six figures Bunny, six figures," he says into the phone.

"I told you I was buying the most expensive." I hold the card he gave me wondering what else I can use it on. I mean, I think my old apartment needs furniture for when I move back. After heading into the furniture store, I order the same bed I slept on last night while he goes on and on with the cost of the dress.

"Why are they asking for your card?"

"I liked your mattress," I tell him.

"Bunny."

"Scratch that, I loved your mattress." I moan.

"My mattress is expensive."

"Oh, I know, I just brought myself one."

"You aren't going back to the spare room." I'm sure his brows are pinched as he holds back his anger.

"Yes, I know. It's for when we divorce. I'll see you later dear." I hang up the phone and call Emma to let her know two mattresses will be delivered today, one for her and me. She sends me back ten smiley faces.

Whiskey isn't home when I arrive, but my dress has already been delivered and is on the bed in the room, and Emma messaged me the mattress got there safe. Going into the kitchen, I start preparing a meal. We haven't actually eaten together. No, the only thing we have shared is sex and drinks.

He calls me Bunny, and he probably thinks I don't know how to cook and that I probably just eat lettuce. Granted, I don't know a lot, as we always had cooks. But Emma's mother is a chef, and on the weekends that I spent with her family, we cooked in the kitchen and her mother would always help me to learn. It was a nice change to being totally ignored.

Making a simple mac and cheese with grilled chicken doesn't take me long. I don't know exactly when he's due home, but it's an easy meal to reheat and it's why I chose it. Just as I sit at his dining room table, I hear his footsteps. When he reaches me, he stops, looks to my plate with scrunched brows, then at me. "You order in?" he asks. I glance at him, and when I do, my eyes narrow. On the white of his dress shirt is red, just droplets, like blood.

"No, I cooked. Yours is still warm in the oven." Going back to my book at the table, I don't wait for his reaction. Not long after his footsteps wander away, I hear the door to the oven open.

"You cooked for me," he says, returning and sitting down next to me. Whiskey places a hand on my book, not the one with red on it though, stopping me from reading. I can't read it anyway with him sitting next to me, I'd be reading the same line over and over again, he's that type of distraction.

"I was hungry. Wasn't sure if you've eaten already, so I cooked." I shrug.

"No one has ever cooked for me before," he

says, making me look up as he starts eating. "Not someone who wasn't getting paid for it, that is."

"Not your parents?" I ask.

"Nope."

"Your wife?" I ask him not believing him.

"Nope, just you."

"Well, then I would suggest you say thank you," I say, taking a mouthful.

"Thank you, Bunny." He moans as he takes a second bite.

He eats it without one complaint, and we don't talk until he's finished. He slides a wedding invite over, and I look at it, trying to hide my smile. It's beautiful. Did I expect anything less though?

We, Whiskey and Lottie, wish to invite you to our celebration of love.

"Do you always sleep naked?" he asks, eyeing me. I look away from the invite and slide it into my book for later, his eyes never leave mine making me feel uncomfortable. His hands are on the table next to his empty plate, and I can't help but look to those hands—just above one is a splotch of red. It has to be tomato sauce, right?

"Do you sleep naked?" I ask, looking up.

He leans over. "Yes. And you would have known if you removed the mountain of pillows when you slept and stopped snoring the house down."

"I don't snore," I argue back.

I like to think I don't, but I know I do.

"Keep telling yourself that. Maybe next time I'll record you and show you."

His words make my spine straighten.

Does he do that often?

Is this some sort of a thing for him?

Whiskey notices my reaction. "It was a joke. I'll never record you again without your permission. I swear," he says.

"I find that hard to believe," I say, trying my hardest to keep the venom from my voice, but it shines through anyway.

"Is there something you want to say to me, Bunny?" he asks, egging me on.

My hands fall to my lap, and I squeeze them tight.

Make him fall in love with me.

Not hate me.

But he seems to like the game we play.

"I said it, did I not?"

Whiskey stands, pushing his seat in, and walks his plate to the sink. I watch from my spot, still seated.

"You're interesting, to say the least, and not quite what I was expecting."

"Were you hoping I'd spread my legs for you every night, to make this arrangement easier for you?"

He laughs at my words. But I can't say that thought hasn't run through my head.

"To be honest, yes. I was hoping for a repeat. But we have a year to build up to that, now don't we?" He smiles as he walks away.

Like I needed that reminder—one long year.

Doing the same thing, I walk into the room and see my dress laying on the bed.

"Tradition doesn't bother you?" he asks, nodding to the dress.

"It's in a bag; you can't see it. Plus, it's not like this is your ordinary wedding where two people love each other."

"True," he says, removing his jacket, and that's when I see more of it.

It's definitely *not* tomato sauce.

Why does he always have to undress around me?

It's entirely unfair and makes this so much

harder than I thought it would be. Because it makes me want him. And I don't want to want him.

"Is that blood?" His eyes fall to where I am pointing, and he just smiles, not giving me an answer. I've heard stories of him, how ruthless he can be.

Picking up my dress, I walk over to him before he can fully undress and push it into his hands.

"Since you like to arrange my things, put this away." Whiskey takes it, because if he didn't, it would drop. He turns around and hangs it up right next to his suits. Taking a deep breath, I start to remove my own shirt, so I'm left only in my black bra. I slide my pants down my legs, leaving only a small G-string wrapped around my body. When I turn around, his eyes are darker and he's watching me with intent.

"I'm showering first." Then I walk into the bathroom, not even bothering to shut the door behind me. After all, he's seen me naked before, fuck, he's kissed and licked every part of me. When I remove the last of my clothing, I notice his reflection in the mirror as he stands at the closet not moving. Quickly showering and getting out, I reach for the towel to see him already there holding it in his hands for me.

"You're playing a game. But Bunny…" His eyes

look up to me, heat is evident in them. "I play better."

Taking the towel from his hand, I step up to him, naked and wet. My body almost brushing his. Whiskey's eyes don't drop. I expect them to. Maybe he's better at this game than I thought.

"Are you sure about that?" His eyes search mine, and then his straight, beautiful white teeth drag over those lips that are begging to be kissed. His warm hand comes to my bare hip, leaving a burning mark in its wake.

His head drops to the side. *Is he thinking about my question?* Then he drags his teeth again over his bottom lip, and I can't look away. He knows it. His hand squeezes my hip and slides a fraction farther down, so he's almost on my ass. Almost. I can feel my body heating and reacting just from his simple touch.

"Are you, Bunny?" he questions.

"We will see, I guess." Pressing myself to him, I lean up so I'm close to his ear, and my breasts are pressed against his chest. "I like to play games. Who better to play them with than my future husband?"

Wrapping the towel around myself, I walk out, shutting the door behind me. The last thing I need is a reminder of how good that man looks naked.

I already know, and it's painful.

But in a very good way.

————

"I know you aren't sleeping." Whiskey is beside me now, has been for a good thirty minutes. I rolled to my side when he laid down, not wanting to look at him and see him naked. It scares me that he may win whatever this game is we're playing at.

And I'm just trying to play when he is probably two steps ahead of me, fuck maybe even ten.

"You don't." I hear him laugh softly next to me.

"You aren't snoring." Turning over, I face him, which is a big mistake because he's already looking at me. "I want to kiss you right now."

"That's good," is all I reply.

"You don't want me to kiss you?" he asks, locking eyes with me.

I'm afraid to blink—will he see my lie if I do?

"No. No, I don't."

"Pity. I could have made it worth your while."

"How?" I ask him.

"How about a month off your contract if you can kiss me like you mean it."

A month?

A whole month.

What is he up to?

Free earlier than I thought would be better than the original contract stated.

"Just a kiss?"

"Just a kiss," he tells me back.

Before I can move to him, his hand touches my lips.

"Make me believe it, Bunny."

I roll my eyes at his words and lock my lips to his.

At first, he doesn't move, and I reach for his wet hair, running my hands through it and moving until he opens his mouth to give me access. When I slide my tongue in, I taste the mint of his toothpaste. His lips smash against mine, and soon we're kissing with sexual tension floating between us so heavy I'm afraid this is just a taste of what's to come. Eleven months will be a long time if we keep this up.

Pulling back, I remove my hand from his hair and look at him. His eyes are closed, and when he opens them, I wait. Wait for what? To see if I can kiss well? Or, to see if he's not a liar?

"That wasn't your best kiss. You didn't make me believe it, Bunny."

My eyes narrow at his words. "I kissed you. Now, you take a month off."

The asshole shakes his head. "No can do! You can have one more chance, though. But this time"—he leans in close, his lips redder from our kiss—"make me believe it."

Make him believe it? Maybe I should punch him in the junk and make him believe that.

Okay, taking a deep breath, I think of how to kiss this man so good that he will take a month off this stupid contract. The sooner I am out of here, the better. As I sit up, I tell myself I'm doing this for one reason only, that this man doesn't make me weak at the knees and causes butterflies to flutter around in my stomach.

No, he makes me sick with the twisted games he likes to play.

Maybe he will be better at this than me.

Whiskey stays where he is, on the other side of the fort I've created. Pushing the pillows away, I climb over to his side so I am straddling his lap and looking down at him. His chest is on display, and I can't help the urge to reach out and touch him, his skin is smooth under my hands—he's all man. You know, to make the kiss as good as it can be, and for no other reason, so I tell myself. Then I run my hands up to his neck leaning down.

I begin by tracing soft kissed along his jawline, continuing until I reach his lips. His hand comes up behind me and touches the small of my back as I stay on him, then I reach up, threading my fingers this time through his hair and pulling it, so when I kiss him, he kisses me back.

Fire. That's all I feel between my legs when we kiss.

Butterflies. They take flight in my belly with a force so fierce they scare me.

But I don't stop.

No, I want this month off, and he isn't bad to kiss. No, I lied, he's magnificent to kiss.

Whiskey hardly touches me, aside from his hand on my back, but that's enough to send me into overdrive. Soon I'm pushing my pelvis down farther, until I can feel him between my legs. He's hard for me, and ready. If only there weren't a sheet and our clothes between us.

Pulling back, I realize his lips are even redder this time, and he's smiling.

"Now that's the kiss." He smirks. "I'll have the contract amended in the morning," he says as I climb off of him. When I do, the blanket comes with me by accident, and in its wake is a naked Whiskey, hard dick and all.

He eyes it then back to me. "If you want to bargain some more..." He winks.

I throw a pillow at him and turn around, forcing myself to sleep and trying to forget all about him.

But that kiss haunts me instead.

CHAPTER 20
WHISKEY

'm not going to be able to get any sleep for a good year. Well, now eleven months. I swear she wakes the dead when she snores.

Looking over at her, my gaze lands on her lips. Those lips are the best fucking lips I have ever had the privilege of touching.

And I can't help but wonder, can I kiss her again?

She was meant to be a means to an end, but I'm almost ready to bargain all eleven months away to have some more of her. It's probably best to avoid her as much as possible until the wedding, afraid of what I might say or do in the meantime is hard.

When she had those legs wrapped around my waist and my cock between her thighs, it was hard to not move that sheet and slide right in. I know what to expect. And I want more of it. Always have. I want her, plain and simple.

"Why are you smirking?" Barry asks, as I'm being fitted for my wedding suit.

"She kissed me last night." I smile telling him.

"Oh fuck, no, Whiskey. What are you thinking?" He shakes his head. "You don't fall for the woman, let her fall for you. It's the way you've planned the game." The tailor looks up to me, most likely confused why I'm being fitted for my own wedding.

"She likes to play. She's fun to play with."

"What if she beats you at your own game?" he asks.

"She won't."

"You can't be too sure of that. She was raised with sharks, remember that."

My smile falls. "I remember exactly who she comes from," I snap back at him.

Barry stands, pushing me away as the tailor starts his suit measurements.

"Okay, just so you know, she isn't worth it, not at all," he says, and a part of me knows and agrees with everything he's saying. But there's one part that isn't sure. She's different from those who she was raised by. I see it, especially when she's around them.

"But her friend, Emma, on the other hand, is for sure worth it." He chuckles.

"Don't fuck her friend." I shake my head, checking my phone.

My personal assistant sent me a message. There's a link which has my name as well as Lottie's.

Recently Divorced Billionaire Set to Marry Senator's Daughter

Then, following the headline is a picture of myself and Lottie from the engagement party. *How the fuck did they get this?* Maybe avoiding her will be harder than I thought.

Smiling, I put the phone to my ear when it rings.

"Bunny."

"Don't you *Bunny* me. Did you see that article? Did you tell the press?"

"No," I answer truthfully. I don't need this to be a big thing. Just enough that her parents believe it's true.

"Fuck! Hold on," she goes, and Barry turns

around to face me, raising an eyebrow. "Okay, looks like Daddy dearest did. Fuck!" She hangs up. Of course he did. If he can have his name in the press, he does it regardless of the cost. He just doesn't want anything bad associated with it.

"What is it?"

"He put a piece out in the paper."

Barry swears. "Well, you did know who you were dealing with."

I nod. I did, but still. His own daughter didn't give him permission.

"I took a month off her contract," I tell him.

"You what?" He shakes his head. "For the kiss, right?" he guesses correctly.

"She should have the papers any minute."

"How long do you plan to play this game?" Barry asks.

"Until I want to stop." I smile.

"Don't invite me to your funeral then."

"You aren't invited."

"Good."

———

Lottie's at home and in bed later that night, and

on my side of the bed is the contract, signed. She doesn't turn as I start to undress and head to the shower. When I come out, she's sitting up with her cell in hand.

"Billionaire's ex-wife says the wedding is a scam. Whiskey Corton is still in love with her, and she can prove it. She also claims to have evidence that he cheated on Miss Snow," she reads, not looking up.

"There's one thing I want to set straight. Right fucking now, asshole. You don't get to touch my business, and that better be in the contract. I bought that all by myself and no one will take it from me." She is gripping the cell as she looks at me.

"Put the phone down. What need would I have for a bar? You know how much money I have, right?"

Lottie does as I ask, then she looks up to me. "You do know how to pick them, right?" she asks, raising an eyebrow.

"I do. I picked you, so I guess I'm doing all right."

She slides back down in bed. "Do you love her? Is she right?"

Dropping my towel, I climb straight into bed, while she watches, not saying a word. "No."

"Have you ever been in love before?"

"I thought I loved her," I tell her honestly. "Have you?"

"I've loved, but I don't think I was in love. My first boyfriend in college."

"It's overrated."

"Is that what you believe?" she asks. "Why?"

"My mother cheated on my father, yet she claimed to love him. Aren't you meant to protect those you love?" I tell her, truthfully.

"I guess, but one bad outcome shouldn't deter you. My grandparents had the greatest love, and one day, I want that for myself," she tells me, and her honesty surprises me.

"You'll get it."

"Just not with you, right?" she says, turning back over and lying down.

"Do you want to play another game?" I ask, avoiding her question.

"No," she answers, not even looking my way.

"This doesn't have to be so painful, you know."

Lottie doesn't answer me.

It's probably for the best.

Who knows what else I might say to her?

Who knows what else she could bargain from me?

————

"Whiskey," Lottie pushes.

I swear I just passed out.

Why is she waking me? I want to sleep.

She pushes me again, kicking me in the leg. "Whiskey."

Opening my eyes, I see her next to me, her hands on my chest, my sheet on the floor.

"You were screaming," she says, her eyes not moving from me, her hand flat on my chest. "What were you dreaming about?" she asks.

Sitting up, I wipe the sweat from my face. "Go back to sleep, Lottie." I climb out going straight to the bathroom, slamming the door shut and leaning against it. Checking the time, it's only been an hour. How the fuck can it only be an hour? I felt like I was trapped in that dream and couldn't escape for hours. I haven't had that nightmare for quite some time. It's been a while since I've seen my father's face, white as a ghost hanging from our garage ceiling.

Standing under the cold water, I let it wash over me hoping it will bring some relief to the hell I was just in.

As I close my eyes to calm my racing heart, I see

him again. I'm not even in bed yet and I already know sleep is not going to be happening tonight.

I turn off the shower, get out, and dry myself off.

Lottie is sitting up, looking at the door. She turns to me when I walk out and climb into bed. "Are you okay?"

"No." Why lie?

"I usually sleep like the dead, but your screams scared me," she says, shivering. "They sounded painful."

"It's over now. Go back to sleep, Lottie."

"Did you need me to do anything?" she asks.

I lie back after switching off the light, and I close my eyes. Her hand finds mine in the pillow fort, and she grips it, then soon, her soft snore fills the room while her hand stays locked in mine. And somehow it feels like a relief to have her there.

I don't let go until the morning.

CHAPTER 21
LOTTIE

Whiskey has avoided me for almost a week. It isn't until the day before our wedding when I come home and he's actually there—at the table with it set up to eat.

"Did you cook?" I ask while sitting. I cooked all week and put his food in the oven every night. The plate was clean each morning when I got up, but he was always gone. If it weren't for that, I would have questioned if he even came home to sleep. A few times, I've woken up in the middle of the night and seen him sleeping next to me. But he's always gone before I wake.

"No, I don't cook, you know that," he says, sliding a glass of water my way.

"Thanks." He nods. "Are you nervous?" I ask him, referring to tomorrow.

"Should I be?"

"I am. I'm getting married. Forced or not, it doesn't matter."

"Only ten and a half months to go, Lottie, then you will be set free."

Eleven months, I read in the contract, started from the date I moved in. The time is getting shorter, and I couldn't be happier about it. If only I didn't have to actually marry him in the first place.

"Why are you here? Isn't it a thing for you to be away from me tonight?" he asks.

"Emma suggested it, but this isn't as real as I would have wanted it to be if I were marrying the love of my life. So why treat it that way?"

He nods. "Fair enough."

"What kind of kiss are we going for tomorrow?" I ask him. That kiss has been on my mind ever since it happened. It needs to go away.

"What one would you like?"

"Fast and quick," I tell him.

Whiskey drags his teeth over his bottom lip, not answering me, then goes back to his food. I play with mine, not sure what else to say to him. He clearly doesn't want to talk about what happened that night.

"How was your day?" he asks finally after he

finishes. A glass of wine comes to his lips, and he looks at me over the brim.

"Is this the game we're playing?" I ask him. "You pretend like this is normal and we're friends? Or what?" My anger's rising.

"It's easier this way, don't you think?"

"Easier for you, or me?" I question him.

"You. It's easier for you."

"Yeah, you keep telling yourself that." I push the plate away. "We are getting married tomorrow, Whiskey. Is this what the next ten or so months is going to look like for me?"

"What's wrong with this?"

"I don't want this. I want my own house. I don't want the first man I live with to only be with me because he wants something from me."

"All men will want something from you. I'm just upfront about it."

"Most don't have a contract and pretend to the world that their marriage is real when it's not."

Whiskey shakes his head and gets up. "I'm ending this conversation. Now." He walks away, and I reach for my glass and throw it near his head. He stops, dropping his plate into the sink. I hear it crack as he turns around to face me.

"No, I'm ending it," I say, smiling as I walk away.

He doesn't let me get too far before he comes up behind me. Whiskey's hand grabs my wrist, and he turns me around. "Ending what exactly?" He presses up against me, and I want to press back and bite his lip at the same time.

"This," I say, pushing on him by accident because I can't move my hands.

Whiskey's head drops into the crook of my neck. "You've been holding my hand every night in your sleep." My spine straightens at his words. "And when you do, your snoring is lighter. Be careful, Bunny, your head may not like me, but some other parts of you most certainly do." He pushes off and beats me into the bedroom.

Taking a few deep breaths, I follow him in. "Who were you dreaming about, Whiskey? What spooked you so bad?"

"My father hanging from my garage ceiling." His back is to me, but I watch as his body tenses.

I didn't expect him to answer. And his words hurt. I can feel the pain even if he doesn't want to show it to me.

"So, you're an asshole to me for what happened back then?"

"Yes, because you're getting too close too soon. Don't deny it, either." He starts undressing.

"Will you stop fucking getting naked around me?"

"I wonder what your father would say hearing you speak like that?" Running my fingers through my hair, I am trying to not pull it out. I really do like my hair.

"I don't care what he would say, I'm speaking to you."

My cell starts ringing, and I ignore it.

"But you do care, don't you? This is why you were the perfect target."

"Target?" I yell at him. "Is that why you picked me? To be your target?" I walk closer to him. His shirt is now off and in his hands.

"Bunny, let's stop. This is going to go nowhere. You and me… It's just a means to an end."

"What end?" I yell.

Whiskey goes to speak, then shakes his head. Undoing his pants, he takes them off and walks into the shower.

I go to the kitchen, grab a bag of flour from the pantry, then walk back into the bedroom, if he thinks he can fuck with me I can do so just as well. Quickly stepping into the en suite bathroom, I grab the laundry basket, turn it over and stand on it. I bring the large bag of flour to my chest, open it, then proceed to empty the contents of the flour all over him. It goes in his mouth, covers his eyes, and when he opens them, I see the mistake I have made by the amount of anger flashing in them. Before I can move, though, he pulls me down from the basket and onto his body. I'm now soaking wet and lying on top of my enemy.

I think my plan may have backfired on me.

"You are on my last nerve, Bunny. I don't have patience for this shit." The flour falls and sticks to his face. It takes everything in me to not laugh out loud. "Oh, you find this funny, do you?" He pushes against me, his cock is hard. My skirt's bunched up, my ass on display. He grips my hips and slides me down. Then I feel him, and the only thing separating us is my flimsy G-string.

My mouth closes, and my smile instantly vanishes.

"Tell me you want me, Bunny. I can ease that ache." I don't speak. "I won't even make you beg for it." He runs his hand up my shirt. I've been with two other men, both around my age, and I'm not sure if it's the age difference or what, but I know he can make any ache that I have between my legs ease. The water washes over my face and stops me from speaking. He leans in and kisses my neck ever so softly. "Tell me, Bunny."

The words are there, on the edge of my lips, so

he pushes a little harder, sliding me down farther and he's right there, and if I pushed and moved the right way, he would be in me. G-string and all.

His kisses pepper my neck, my jawline, and hands roam my back.

I'm marrying this man tomorrow. Whiskey will be my husband, and I want to fuck him. But the words won't leave my mouth, and I'm glad they won't, even if they are on the tip of my tongue.

"You taste like everything sweet. I remember the way you taste." Whiskey pushes just a fraction. A gasp leaves my mouth. "Do you remember how I taste, Bunny? How my cock filled your mouth as you wrapped those sweet lips around it?" He pauses, sucks on my neck. "I do. Fuck, I do. You give the best head." His words are hypnotizing me. I'm trying to break free, to not fall for them. But when his mouth covers mine, I open for him. He doesn't take my kiss straight away, he simply tastes me, and I can taste him mixed in with the flour I poured all over him.

Damn. He's using me.

Is this me using him as well?

I'm so confused.

Should I be having sex with my fake husband? The man who is also my blackmailer and using me in his big plan of revenge. Is this normal?

"Kiss me, Bunny."

I do, my hands come up and grip his face as he holds me in place. His chest pushes against my breasts, holding me still. My lips part, and I take control of the kiss. He lets me. Whiskey pulls away from my entrance, and his cock comes to rub on my clit, up and down as our tongues dance a dance they're familiar with.

I've never had this much passion or attraction for a man before.

Never wanted someone, and not wanted someone, all at the same time.

Our lips pull away, we both breathe heavily, then he pushes me against the wall. His hands leave my back, and they search my body. Roaming me as if he's figuring me out.

My mind is telling me to stop this.

For god's sake, don't have sex with him.

But my body is screaming for relief.

Whiskey was the last man I slept with. I haven't been with anybody since him, and I want him again. Very badly.

Pushing on his chest, I find he goes back with ease.

Face rigid, he looks up at me, long eyelashes with flour on them wait for me to speak.

Taking a few deep breaths, I stand and pull my

skirt back down. I let my eyes drop to his chest, which is hard and all muscle and dusted with a smattering of hair. That perfect V he has showcases his cock ever so beautifully, like it's ready to explore my vagina.

His cock's so hard and angry and waiting for me to invite it in.

My vagina throbs at the thought.

I know I want him.

But should I do so? How do I keep my dignity intact?

I look back up at him. "If you want me, this isn't the right way to have me," I say.

I have to play a game as well. The same one he plays with me.

Deception.

"What's the right way to make both our troubles"—he looks down at my pussy—"disappear." My mouth opens. "I know you want me just as badly as I want you, rich girl. I can smell you."

"You want to fuck me the day before our wedding?" I ask him.

Whiskey nods his head. "I don't care what day it is. And yes, I want to fuck you." He looks down. "It's pretty obvious, isn't it?"

My eyes follow his.

"I'll hate you even more if we do this."

"Get out," he says, shaking his head and turning around in the shower.

I do as he says, stepping out and taking his towel with me.

Turning back to look at him, I see his head on the tiled wall as the water rushes over his back, washing the flour down the drain—and any hopes I had with it.

CHAPTER 22
WHISKEY

I know what game she's playing at. That woman thinks she can change my viewpoint of her. Make me see her for more than what she really is—a rich girl who has had everything handed to her in this life. Well, she's wrong.

I see her, and I've been playing way longer than she has.

Walking out, she's sitting on the bed with her cell in hand.

"This house will be yours after the wedding. I'm going to my apartment," I tell her my plan.

I have needs, and my future wife won't meet them, no matter how much she teases me.

"What?" She looks at me, shocked. "You're just leaving me in this house?" she questions.

"Yes. It will make things easier. My office is closer to my apartment anyways."

Lottie throws a pillow at my face. I catch it.

"Sometimes you act like a spoiled brat," I say to her, throwing the pillow to the floor.

"That's rich coming from you. You can't function if you are not getting your way. First, you blackmail me. Then you force me to marry you. You made me move in here. Made me give up my home. So, you can what…" Her eyebrows raise. "Move into your own apartment?"

"Yes."

"Why?"

"It's easier that way. You can have this house to yourself. Some of my things will still be here to show that I am living here, but I won't be. You can do as you please, just don't ruin my clothes again."

"So tomorrow, you're just going to go to your apartment?"

"Yes, we've just discussed this."

"So, you can fuck who you want. Correct?"

I smile. She isn't dumb.

"Yes."

"Thank fuck, I didn't just fuck you then." She turns around, showing me her back as she turns off the light.

"Goodnight," I tell her.

"Fuck off already," she tells me back.

———

"Okay, dude, there's over one hundred people out there. What the fuck?" Barry says, opening the door and coming back inside. "This was meant to be small."

It was, until her father got involved and changed all our plans.

"Is it time?" I ask him.

Lottie didn't speak to me this morning. She simply took her dress out of the closet when her friend Emma arrived and left without saying good-bye. It's probably easier that way. Not to have to deal with her attitude or mood swings. After this, she can go on living her life, and we will only have to be together for functions, so people believe we are actually husband and wife.

Easy.

I hope.

The door opens, and in walks her father dressed in a designer suit.

"You ready?" he asks, looking from me to Barry, who's nodding his head.

"Yes."

"Good. She's ready," he says, looking behind him. "Did you think any more about my offer of the sponsorship?"

Barry looks to me, knowing full well what type of man this is we are dealing with.

"No, not yet."

"Okay, well, think on it. We have a gala coming up soon. It could benefit you." He spins around and walks out.

"Did he just do that on your wedding day?" Barry asks. "That man is a real piece of work."

"Yep."

"How on earth did Lottie even manage to turn out normal with him around."

It isn't a question. It's a fact.

She should be a ruthless cold-hearted bitch, and in some ways, she is. But I can also see she cares. Something her father lacks greatly. He doesn't even show his daughter affection unless it's fake and in public so he can gain from it. I bet he didn't even ask her if she loves me. He's just happy that she's marrying someone of quality for money.

"Okay, let's do this."

Barry straightens out his suit jacket and walks out, I follow closely behind until I am standing at the end of the aisle. I had the venue picked out already and let her decorate it to her tastes.

Though, my assistant told me Lottie said she could do whatever the fuck she wanted with it. So, I have a feeling she has no idea, and she probably couldn't care less either.

Either side of the aisle is green, with logs covered in moss. It's very outdoorsy but has an inside feel. Flowers coat the floor where she will be walking, and fairy lights drop down on either side of the aisle.

It is beautiful.

The music starts playing, and soon everyone stands.

My hands start to sweat.

Is this really the best thing to do?

I should call it off.

I don't want to get married again.

Fuck!

Looking back, I hear the invited guests gasp, and then I see her.

Holy shit! She's beautiful.

Lottie has on an open form dress, where it goes up the front to a skirt and falls at the back with a train, her legs have rhinestones all over them, and her feet are bare as she steps on the flowers covering the floor.

Her hair is tied up, and her face is even more beautiful with a little makeup applied.

Lottie's lips are red as fire, and she smiles when she sees me, making me in turn smile back at her. I can tell it's forced, but mine isn't.

She really is the most beautiful woman I've ever seen. I don't even look at her father when she reaches me, placing her hand in mine. My eyes don't leave hers. It is next to impossible to do so. How could they treat her this way?

"You look beautiful," I tell her, and it's the truth.

"Thank you," she says back to me.

The ceremony starts, and my hand doesn't leave hers. Her dress clings to her upper body like it was painted on her. It shows no cleavage as it wraps around her neck.

Everything goes fast and in a blur. The whole time, I can't stop looking at her. She blushes at my stare and does well to hide it.

Then when those words are spoken, I know I'm about to go back on my word. That the kiss won't be small. I need to taste her again like I need my next breath.

"You may kiss the bride."

She turns to me, and I inch forward, grabbing her neck with one hand and the other goes on her back. I drop her down, kissing her lips. She doesn't open her mouth at first, thinking it will be just that, a small kiss, but I need more, and she *will* give it to me because people are watching, and we are now husband and wife.

So, I take full advantage of it. I can taste her lipstick, but what's better is her. Lottie finally gives me access, and our tongues do a dance all of their own. People start cheering, and she pushes at my chest until I bring her back up. Looking down, our hands are joined, and I see the rings that are on our fingers.

Two unlikely people tied together from her father's mistakes.

I bet she never saw me in her future.

But I'm very glad I'm in it.

CHAPTER 23
LOTTIE

Whiskey's hand stays in mine while we walk the aisle, but the minute we are out, I pull it free and walk over to the closest room with a door to get away from him. He lets me go, and when I check my face, I see the red lipstick smudges everywhere. Washing it off, I reapply so any evidence of him is now gone.

"Lottie."

Taking a deep breath, I ignore him.

How dare he kiss me like that in front of all those people?

Who does he think he is?

I want to junk-punch him. Hard.

"Just get it over with and come out and yell at me. We need to make our entrance in five minutes."

Flinging the door open, he's leaning on the back

of a couch. His arms crossed over his chest, watching me.

"You didn't get permission to kiss me like that." I'm fuming. "How dare you!" I scream.

"You look beautiful. Did I tell you that? Prettiest bride I have ever seen." His words hit me, and I try to not let them affect me. They shouldn't be able to. I'm mad at him.

They do.

"Stop it," I say.

Whiskey smirks, pushes off the couch, and walks over to me. His hands come out and grab mine.

"I'm so mad at you," I tell him. "But my makeup is perfect, and I look too good to cry right now."

His smirk grows to a full smile. "That's true, you are." He leans in and kisses my cheek. "It's almost over. I promise I won't kiss you like that again."

And I believe him.

He's doing exactly what I've asked.

So why does this all hurt a little?

"At least the non-believers now believe," I say, shrugging.

"They do. And what's not to believe?" He winks, taking my hand.

"Let's go out there."

We start walking to the door, and just before he pulls it open, he says, "I'm glad it was you, just so you know." Then he opens the door, and we walk out and into our reception. The reception is set up much the same as the ceremony. Flowers and greenery lay everywhere with twinkling fairy lights hanging like rain from the ceiling.

"I think I need to hire your personal assistant for myself," I tell him. She's impressive.

I spot her, and she's the first person we walk over to.

"Thank you for this." Her face goes red at my words. "Whiskey has a huge bonus for you as a thank you."

Whiskey says nothing, so I elbow him. "Yes, of course," he says through gritted teeth.

She smiles brightly as we leave her.

"Sneaky," he says, leaning down to my ear.

People start cheering as we walk farther inside and take our seats at the bridal table. Soon the food starts to come out, and I turn to Emma who's watching me.

"So, that kiss. You two do that often?" she whispers.

"No." Then I remember. "Okay, last night."

Her mouth drops. "Lottie, are you sure that's smart?"

"He's moving into his apartment. I'll have the house to myself until it's done."

"Wow! Really?"

I shrug. "So, he says."

"Well, I've been trying to get more info from Barry. But the man's impossible. He almost let something slip, but then shut up and changed the subject."

"Are you sleeping with him?" I ask, realizing I haven't been seeing her as much as I usually do.

"Ummm…" She pulls at the fabric of her dress.

"Emma, really? Sleeping with the enemy," I say while shaking my head.

"He's fun, and he's good."

We both turn to look at him as he sits next to Whiskey, and when he sees us staring, he winks before turning back to speak with Whiskey.

"Okay, just remember who's side you're on."

She taps her hand on mine. "Yours, of course. I'm just taking one for the team." She giggles.

"Congrats."

We both turn to Clinton who's standing in front of us, his eyes moving over to me then to Whiskey. "Congrats." He holds up his drink, then takes a sip.

"Thank you," I reply.

"You two really are a thing, huh? That kiss…" He shakes his head and looks to me, I never enjoyed kissing him. "I assumed it was all a lie."

Emma's hand touches mine under the table.

"But that kiss," he says again, looking from my lips to Whiskey. "You're a lucky man."

"That I am," Whiskey says back to him as he leans over and kisses my temple.

Clinton walks off after that.

"Someone wants what I have."

I shiver. I hated being kissed by Clinton.

"Too bad you blackmailed me for it," I whisper, so only the people at the table can hear. Barry looks to me then turns away.

"At least you don't have to deal with Clinton anymore. That's a win, is it not?"

"I can handle him," I say.

"I'm sure you can," he patronizes me.

"When is this over? When can I leave?"

The waiter slides my food in front of me.

"At least until dessert, darling," he says in a sweet voice as the waiter places Whiskey's food down in front of him.

"Thank god," I say, turning away from him and back to Emma.

"The tension is thick," she whispers to me,

giggling. "You should just fuck him and get it over with."

I smack her arm. "No. Don't suggest that."

Wiggling her eyebrows, she says, "How are you meant to make him fall in love with you then?"

Before I can answer, my parents walk up to the table and are standing in front where Clinton was before. "Congratulations," my mother says, and my father nods. "Where will you be going for your honeymoon?"

I look to Whiskey.

Oh shit! That wasn't discussed. I don't want one of them.

"We aren't. Not yet at least. Lottie can't leave the bar."

My mother's eyes train in on me. "Well, how about you take our lake home for a few days?"

"No," I say it too fast, and my father's eyes narrow in on me. "Whiskey's right, I don't have the time to take off at work. We will do something, just the two of us, when the time is right," I reply, leaning into him.

His hand goes straight to my thigh, but I shake it off.

"Well, make sure you mingle with your guests," my father says.

Of course he would say that.

I can barely contain the eye roll I so badly want to unleash in this moment. Not once when I was ready to walk down the aisle did he ask me if this was what I wanted or was I okay to do this.

He was happy with who I was marrying, and that's all he cares about. To be honest, it made me mad. Even though, as a child, I wanted to please him. And even as an adult, I still do. I shouldn't have to sacrifice everything in my life for him. Which is what I'm doing right now.

"We can go," Whiskey whispers.

I turn to Emma. "Come over later? Or tomorrow?" I ask her.

She looks past me to Barry, then back to me. "Tomorrow."

I smile, but it's forced. I was hoping she would say tonight and maybe even stay with me.

Someone who I don't recognize walks over and leans down to Whiskey's ear, whispers something then walks off.

"If you'll excuse me."

"Where are you going?" I ask him, he just smiles and walks outside. I sit at the table watching the door like a hawk, guests are mingling and eating, Barry and Emma are talking over me on either side of the table as I sit there and wait. The music changes and someone says something to me, but I don't answer as he walks in. He wipes his hands as he walks closer to me, and when he sits, I look at the towel he was using and see blood.

That's the second time I have seen blood on him.

Why?

"Where did you go?"

He just smirks, and when he does, I see the thing I've heard about Whiskey—that while he is an amazing businessman, he is also very, very deadly.

"That was blood," I whisper. He stands, I do the same. We walk out for our first dance; he grips me to him and pulls me in tight. His hands on my waist.

"Why was there blood?" I ask him.

"Do you want the truth?" I nod, and he leans in so close that his chin is on my neck.

"I just killed someone who thought they could sneak around on me, right now my men are removing his body."

I pull back, the shock on my face. He laughs, leans in, and kisses me on the lips. I know people are watching so I kiss him back quickly and pull away. He follows, and we go outside the cold air hitting me.

"Did you really just kill someone?"

He smirks.

"Of course I did, usually that's my men's job, but I had to blow off some steam like the old days. Who the fuck did you think you were marrying?" I stand there, unable to say a word. "Goodnight, wife."

He shuts the door behind me.

And I'm left standing at our wedding, in my wedding dress, all alone.

———

Emma comes over as planned, and then she comes the next day as well, until she has to go back to work. I, on the other hand, have taken the week off. That, as it stands, was probably a mistake. I should have gone straight back to work, instead of living this life. His life, in his house.

What kind of life is this going to be? Not one I chose, that's for sure, at least I still have my business.

My week consists of me hanging around the house watching Netflix and ordering as much bad takeaway as I can fit in my stomach.

Not once do I see or hear from him.

The weeks start to fall away fast once I return to work.

It's been close to a month now since I've seen Whiskey, since we've been married, and I'm glad it's going fast, but it's a lonely existence. I hate this house and being stuck in it.

When my father pops around for unexpected visits, which he's done twice, I lie telling him Whiskey's at work, when in reality I have no idea where he is.

Today though, today's a good day.

We have a band booked, and recently they hit number one worldwide.

"I would offer to buy you a drink..." I turn to the lead drummer of one of America's biggest bands. Shane's hair is long, his lip pierced, and in his mouth hangs a cigarette. Not lit.

"Sorry?" I say confused.

He isn't talking to me, is he?

"You're beautiful, and I want to take you out. Where should we go?" he asks me. The rest of the band members look my way, and my face reddens.

"I'm married," I say, spitting it out and hating myself for it.

"But...are you?" Shane steps closer, smelling like cigarettes and bad regrets.

I want him.

Why do I want him?

Is it because I am craving a touch from someone else?

Shane is at the end of the bar, nothing's separating us. Only a glass which I'm holding in my hand.

His band members start to leave my bar, leaving just the two of us here by ourselves. Shane reaches for my hand, turns it over, and pulls a pen out of my pocket that I use for writing food orders. When he's done, he blows on it and steps back.

"Call me when you think you aren't married. But believe me, I have no qualms about sleeping with a married woman." Shane winks and walks out.

My heart beats loudly in my chest as he goes, and I have to remember to breathe.

The last man I was attracted to is now my husband.

Now, I'm way wary of who to let in. *Could they fuck me over as well?*

Maybe record me to?

I hate Whiskey for putting those insecurities inside of me. I never had them before him and his bullshit.

After closing up, I head home, constantly looking at my hand. I shouldn't do it. I know it would be wrong. I'm a married woman, and I'm not a cheater. I have strong beliefs in that. But is it cheating if it's fake? The certificate might be real, but the marriage is anything but.

Pulling up to my home—technically his home—I notice his car is parked in the garage.

What on earth is he doing here?

Wondering if I should pull away and come back later or just go in, I decide to go in, because this can't be my life avoiding the asshole. I need to face him head-on.

Gathering all my strength, I pull my jacket on and walk inside. When I do, he's sitting at the dining room table with food, waiting for me, as if he hadn't left.

"Whiskey."

He turns to face me. His eyes roam me as I walk closer to him.

Pulling out a seat, I sit across from him. "Why are you here?"

"To see you, of course," he answers.

"Why?" He pushes a plate toward me full of food.

"Can I not visit my wife?" he asks.

I watch him for motive. He's here for something. What? I just don't know yet. I look down at my hand, the one with Shane's number on it. I was thinking of calling him. Maybe.

"What's that on your hand?" Whiskey's eyes glance down, and I pull my hand away and place it under the table.

"What do you want?"

"What's on your hand?"

"A number," I answer him truthfully.

"Who's number?"

"A drummer."

"Name?"

"Shane," I answer.

He nods. "And do you plan to fuck him?"

Whiskey's words for some reason shock me. "Get out."

I get up from the table, not even bothering to go any further with this conversation.

Whiskey follows me though.

Because he can't leave well enough alone.

CHAPTER 24
WHISKEY

"You should check your phone." I smile as I hit send to her. She eyes me suspiciously and reaches for her phone pulling it out, when she does, I know what she sees.

Did she really think I wouldn't know. She has a drummer's number on her hand, and I saw it happen, I watched as she paused and I could tell, if I was not in the picture, she would have gone home with him that night.

"You are recording me again?" she screams and throws her phone at my head. "How did you get cameras in my bar? How do you even have access to the cameras in my bar? Fuck you, Whiskey." She walks over and pushes me, but I don't budge.

I lean in real close.

"Those cameras are mine."

"They are not," she says her hand goes to her hip at it pops to the side.

Fuck, this woman.

"Oh, but they are. I watch you strut your stuff in that bar. I watch as men eye fuck you. But you are married now. So, I won't accept it. He's lucky I didn't break his fucking legs for what he said, and if you call him, Bunny, I will break his fucking legs."

"You don't have the power, just because you are rich doesn't mean you have that power." I smile and lean in and kiss her cheek, she sucks in a breath.

"I've killed for less, my sweet Bunny."

Lottie storms off to the bedroom, and when I walk in, I don't even recognize it as my own anymore. All my things are gone from the closet, and all that hangs in there are her things. Her wedding dress, which I dream about her in often, hangs proudly on the door.

"You got rid of my things?" I ask, coming up behind her.

She starts taking off her earrings, one by one. "Yes. Why would I keep your shit here if you aren't here," she answers, then sits on the bed, slipping off her shoes.

"Don't get undressed. We have an event."

She eyes me up and down. "You can go by your damn self."

"No, you should come. Your parents will be there."

She harrumphs, and I know I've won.

"Black tie?" she asks, but the way she says it I can see the defeat in her. Then with an eye roll she follows with, "Of course, it is. My father would not go to anything less." She walks to her closet and pulls out a dress.

"You don't have to wear an evening dress, if you don't want to."

She eyes me suspiciously. "What? Of course I do, there's a dress code for a reason." Then she starts undressing.

I turn, looking away and sitting on the bed while she gets ready.

Walking into the bathroom she disappears, and I see the bedding has even changed. You can't even tell I used to live here. It's completely her.

"Okay, I'm ready. Let's get this over with." Lottie didn't redo her make-up, but she still looks absolutely beautiful.

"Your father has asked me again. He's very keen for me to sponsor him."

"You do what you want, like you do anyway.

Honestly, I couldn't care less." She grabs her purse and starts to walk to my car, so I open the door for her as she climbs in.

Leaning down, I look at her green eyes. They're vibrant tonight, and I wonder if it's Shane who put the sparkle there, and then I wonder if it's me who will continue to dim it. "You should care." Then I shut the door.

Walking around, I slide into the car. We go in complete silence. I probably should have started the conversation with 'how have you been?' instead of interrogating her. But I can't help myself. I had to know. I keep tabs on her, and she leads a pretty simple life. It's one she seems to enjoy—work, friends, and home. Guys notice her, but she doesn't notice them.

Until tonight.

Arriving at the venue, a red carpet is set up, and I smile.

"Is this a large function?" she asks, looking at the venue.

"Yes."

She sighs but puts on the fakest of smiles as I walk around to her door and help her out. She places her hand in mine as the cameras start flashing as we walk toward the entrance, "at least they make it obvious they are recording." Dropping her hand at her words, I place mine on the small of her back, she stiffens at my touch when we walk in.

When you've been to one of these, you've been to them all. And they eventually become redundant and lose the appeal they once held. Now, I'd rather be anywhere but here. I would rather be sitting at an IHOP with this woman on the other side of the table.

"You made it," Barry exclaims. "And you look beautiful, Lottie." He nods to her.

She offers him a small smile, then turns away from him.

"Business first," Barry says to me. "If you will excuse us, Lottie, your father is over near table one." Barry nods for me to follow him, and when I do, I turn around to see her not moving. Looking where her eyes are currently affixed, I stop.

"Man, come on," Barry says, noticing I've stopped.

"Can't." I turn back just as the dude from the bar reaches her. Her smile is big. Overly large. I haven't had a smile like that from her, ever. Shane reaches for her hand, kisses it on one side, and offers her a crooked smile. I should be the bigger man and let her go. Let her have a chance to actually fall in love.

But I'm a cruel son of a bitch, and I don't want to share.

Not yet anyway.

Shane drops her hand as I walk up behind her. Lottie doesn't notice me, but he does. He straightens and the smirk that he held for her drops too. He doesn't know me, but when I touch Lottie's back, he gets the message, and she flinches at my touch.

"The husband?" Shane asks, looking back to Lottie.

Who now looks angry, and it's mixed with sadness.

"The husband indeed, and you are?" Shane offers me his hand, but I don't take it.

"Shane. You got a keeper here, man. And a fine bartender at that." He nods to Lottie, and when he does, she blushes and then smiles, and it touches her eyes.

"I know I do. But I'm sure anyone can pour a drink."

Shane looks at me in surprise.

My hand stays put on Lottie's back, and I can feel that she stops breathing.

"Lottie, you remember what I said."

She nods, and Shane winks as he walks away.

She pushes away from my hand, so I am no longer touching her.

"Was that the part where he would want to fuck a married woman?"

Lottie looks everywhere around the room before she speaks. Her eyes are angry, fiery, but a fake smile stays in place. Perfect.

"He still wants me. Yet I'm married to you and can't even get a reaction out of you. Well not one that I should be getting from my husband." She turns, then looks back to me. "And if you degrade what I do for a living again, I'll make you regret you ever opened your overly large mouth. Asshole." Then she walks off over to her parents. Her father greets her as if she isn't his daughter but a business venture. Her mother kisses each cheek, but not once does she touch her. It's the fakest family I have ever seen. And that's saying a lot living where I live.

"Man, you spoke to Shane. Holy shit. He's an amazing drummer, the best actually."

"That might be, but he's a dick, and I may very well bury him ten feet under the fucking ground if he goes near her again." Barry shakes his head. "You can't kill the drummer," Barry says, making me turn to face him.

"So, you want to fuck my wife as well?" I ask.

"What?" He looks at me, puzzled. "I mean, if she's offering."

I shake my head when he laughs.

"Shane wants to fuck your wife. Well shit! Shane usually gets what he wants."

We both turn to look at her and watch as she checks around and then she spots Shane. Her smile is back in place, and we watch as he winks at her.

"You're fucked. I'm not even gay, and I would fuck Shane." Barry laughs.

"That shit's not helping, maybe I'll break his legs tonight so he will stop eye fucking her."

"What do you mean, you idiot. You moved on. You said you didn't want her. That's why you haven't seen her for well over a month, right? Clean break. That's what you said." He repeats my words right back to me.

"Maybe I was out of line."

"No. No way. Leave her be, man. You've already fucked with her enough."

He's right, but my head is telling me to take her. I want her, there's no denying that fact at all.

"No can do." Walking back over, her eyes fall to mine, and she looks away. She's been caught, and she knows it. Looking his way, I see Shane watching us.

I place my hand on her back again as I lean

down to whisper in her ear. "We can fuck, and I'll make you forget all about him. After, I'll go and break his legs."

Oh, my god. The look to kill. The pure venom, it's leaching out of her. She wants to swear at me, I know she does. Actually, I think if that perfectly perfect persona wasn't firmly in place she would reach out and head-butt me into the middle of next week.

But her father speaks, "Whiskey, so good to see you. Let me introduce you to some friends." Her father waves at me to follow.

Lottie doesn't look my way when I leave her again.

CHAPTER 25
LOTTIE

"So, he's possessive of you," Shane says, coming up behind me.

Somehow, I managed to escape after listening to my mother talk dresses for the last ten minutes and driving me crazy with her designer bullshit. Whiskey is off frolicking with the rich, which I guess is what he does. But I have felt his eyes on me the whole time. Even when he thought I didn't notice.

"Who?" I ask, turning as Shane pulls a cigarette out from behind his ear and leans on the balcony. I stay near the door but still outside, too afraid to look over, but needing the fresh air and the escape. "Did you follow me out here?" I ask him, smiling and looking behind me to make sure my husband didn't see—eww that word "husband" feels bad in my mind. Is that what he is? I guess legally he is.

"I did. And your husband. He hasn't been able to keep his hands and eyes off you. Tell me, Lottie, do you want him?" I feel my cheeks redden at his words.

"No." And the minute that leaves my mouth, I cover it with my hands.

He smirks. Lights his cigarette. "I figured as much. There's tension there. But I don't know what kind," he says as if he has it all figured out. "But I can tell he wants you at the very least."

I shrug because I shouldn't answer that. I go through waves of wanting and hating Whiskey. Lately, it's been all about hating. But when I see him, no matter how mad he makes me, I still want him. *Why is that?*

"Did you keep my number?" I look down at my hand for some reason, knowing it washed off.

"Pass me your phone."

I do, and he types his number in and smiles when he hands it back to me.

"Booty call?" I ask him, reading it and looking up to him.

"Anytime. Anywhere." Shane moves over, leans down, and kisses the side of my lips. I can smell the cigarette that still lingers on his lips as he leaves and have to remember to breathe.

My heart rate finally slows down as I close my eyes and dream. Dream of a life that I was living before this nightmare began.

"He only wants you because you're married." I jump, not expecting someone to be there, and my phone drops to the floor. Thankfully it doesn't smash. Leaning down, Whiskey picks up my phone and turns it around. "Booty call," he reads out. "He has some nerve, let me tell you that, luckily for him he doesn't need his legs to be a drummer."

"Luckily for you, this marriage is fake," I say, reaching for my phone and sliding it back into my purse.

"Touché." He nods.

"I can fuck whoever I want, the same as you. Don't think you'll be the only one having fun, husband." I push past him to leave.

Whiskey stops me, our shoulders touching as he leans over. "But it's me you wish was fucking you. Isn't it, wife? I could fuck you right here, right now. Cover your mouth with mine to stop those screams I know you make."

My angry eyes turn to him. "You would know, you have it all on video for your viewing pleasure," I fire back at him.

He smirks then drags his teeth over his bottom lip. "Why deny what's between us? You have an itch that needs to be scratched, and so do I."

"I bet yours has been scratched and sucked lately," I fire back.

"Surprisingly, no. But if you're offering..." He looks me over then leans down to kiss me, but I turn just in time as his lips touch the side of my face. His kisses fuck me over and make me putty in his hands, and that fact is entirely unfair.

"Your wife doesn't like to be fucked by liars and manipulators," I remind him.

"You had no trouble last time," he says with a click of his tongue.

I lean close to him, so it seems I might kiss him. "I didn't realize who I was getting into bed with, go figure. Now I see you, know you, I don't want you."

Whiskey's hand makes me jump when it touches my dress. "I can smell you. You're an awful liar. What if I inched up farther, would you be wet right now?" His hand moves and I make no move to stop him.

"Yes," I breathe, not even bothering to lie.

Then I reach up on my tippy toes and whisper in his ear, "But it's not for you." Then I pull away and return to the party.

———————

Whiskey leaves me alone for at least an hour. The party is starting to slow down, and some people have left, Shane being one of them. When the band left, I wished I could have gone with them.

We are walking out, it's time to leave. This time, Whiskey doesn't touch me, which is a relief.

"You two should come over for dinner soon. Do you have any other family, Whiskey?" my father asks him as we wait for the valet to bring his car around, knowing full well both of his parents are dead.

"No, just Lottie." He touches me again, and damn, it really is a struggle not to pull away.

"Well, now you have us as well. How fabulous," my mother says.

I smile at her words because I know they're fake.

"Yes. How fabulous," Whiskey mimics my mother.

"Dinner is settled then, tomorrow at seven. Just a small gathering with the family." He taps Whiskey's back a few times. "That's what families do."

Whiskey nods. It's funny watching the two of them standing next to each other. On one hand, you have Whiskey. Tall. Impeccable hair. On the other hand, you have my father. No hair, much shorter than Whiskey. I wouldn't say he's out of shape, but you can begin to see the roundness that has settled at his core. My father used to pride himself in his appearance, but the years of stress have started to creep in on him.

"We would love to," he answers for us.

"Actually, I have a band booked tomorrow, and I'm opening…" I pause, staring at my father. "Shane's band, you know them?

"Oh yes," he says, as I see Whiskey's eyes narrow at me. "You have to attend to those famous people. We all know how demanding they can be."

"Hopefully, very demanding," I say, smiling.

My father shakes his head and waves us good-bye, but when I turn to face Whiskey anger swims all over his face.

"Demanding?" He leans in. "Do you want *me* to be demanding?" Whiskey's car pulls up in front of us and the door is opened for me. I slide in without replying to him.

He walks around to his side, jumps in, and then takes off like an idiot. Whiskey hits the gas hard, so much so that I have to hold on to the side of the door. He doesn't head in the direction of his house where I'm living, instead he drives like a lunatic toward the city, pulling into an underground parking garage. Whiskey gets out and walks around to my side, opening the door and holding it for me.

"Come now, Bunny."

"This isn't where I'm staying." He drops his hand, his shirt slightly open revealing tanned, taut skin.

"It is tonight. Seems when you make me mad, I want you even more."

"You can't have me," I argue back staying in the car.

"That's the thing, though, isn't it? We want what we can't have." Then he offers me his hand, and I take it but I'm not sure why.

"I need to go. I'll order an Uber."

"No, you won't. You will stay here."

"In your whore house?" I say with a wave of my hand.

Whiskey laughs as he pushes the button for the elevator. "This is my private apartment. No one stays here."

"So, where have you been fucking your whores then?"

We walk in and he shakes his head. "Do you want him?"

I know who he's talking about, but I play dumb anyway. "Who?"

The elevator starts moving, and Whiskey pushes me against the wall, backing me into the corner. He touches a piece of hair, pushing it back from my face. "Shane. Do you want him?"

"Yes," I breathe, my heart rate rising at the thought, and also from Whiskey touching me.

"You should have said no."

"Why?"

"Because now I hate him, and Barry won't like that."

I shake my head. "You can get off of me now."

"On you?" He pushes on me. "I'm sure I heard you correctly."

"You like to play games with me, don't you, Whiskey?"

He leans in so he's near my ear. "Say it again."

"What?"

"My name."

"Asshole." I try to push him back, but he doesn't move. He chuckles, and the vibration runs through me. The elevator grinds to a halt, the door dings and opens. He pushes off me and reaches for my hand, pulling me through the door.

Penthouse. Of course, he has a penthouse.

Should I have really expected anything less from him?

Once inside, I stop. "I can't believe an asshole like you would have such a beautiful place." His hand drops from mine when I see the first picture hanging on the wall. "You all look so happy," I say, smiling at the photograph of him and his family.

"We were. Or so I believed."

"She's beautiful, your mother."

His lip turns up. "She's selfish," is all he replies.

"You were close to your father, but not her?"

Whiskey doesn't tell me much, and to be honest, I never really cared to ask. But I can see this place is truly his, compared to the one I'm currently staying in.

"Yes, she was an unnecessary evil."

"Did he remarry?"

"No, he loved her to his dying breath. The damn idiot." He shakes his head. "This was his place, now it's mine."

"Why the other place?"

"I bought it after I met you."

"With the intention of me living there?" I ask.

"Yes. You needed somewhere where it wasn't in my personal space."

"You put me in the same room as you," I say defensively.

He shrugs. "I like the way you smell."

My mouth falls open and my nose turns up. "You didn't just say that."

Whiskey's eyes roam over me. "I didn't say what smell." He wiggles his eyebrows. Then he walks off. I follow him through the dark hallway that leads to a gleaming white kitchen with stainless steel appliances. Two stools sit on one side of the kitchen counter.

Whiskey heads to the fridge and pulls out a beer. "Are you avoiding drinking around me still, or would you like one?"

I haven't had a drink in months, avoiding it has been necessary after what happened last time. After all, I am still paying for that gigantic mistake.

"Are you planning on recording me again?" I ask.

"No. The only cameras in here are the ones at the entry. Unless you want to stand in the entry and strip…" he raises an eyebrow in question, "… then no. But I wouldn't mind a strip show… for my eyes only."

With a sigh, I walk over and take the beer from his hand then sit on the stool.

"That's my girl."

"I'm not your damn girl."

"Your ring and last name tell me otherwise."

"I didn't change it."

"But you did on Facebook."

"Yes, because that's what matters," I say with an eye roll and sarcasm dripping from my words.

"To your father, it does."

I take a sip of the beer, it tastes good. I've missed the bitter taste. "Why am I here, Whiskey?"

He comes around and sits next to me, turning so his body is facing mine. "It's hard to stay away from you." His words hit me hard. "And I seem to become extremely jealous with you."

"You have nothing to be jealous of," I reply, and he smiles. "I was never yours to begin with."

His smile drops. "We could have some fun. Why won't you have some fun with me?"

"What kind of fun?"

"Sex," he states.

"With you?" I raise an eyebrow.

"Yes. No one else."

"What do I get?" I ask, even though I'm ready to say yes. I'm a weak woman right now, and I really do want sex, but I may as well get something out of it. Is it classed as selling myself when it's something I want?

"I'll take another month off," he says quickly.

"A whole month for you to have my body, just once?"

"No. Every week."

"Every week," I say, sitting back. "Eager much?"

"I was going to try for every day, but figured I was pushing my luck."

"So, only eight months left then. If I agree, that is."

"Yes."

"Let's add in some clauses, shall we?" I take another sip of my beer.

"You sleep with anyone else… it is off. No more sex. And you will not come on to me at all or touch me inappropriately." He nods. "Two, if I don't want to, you can't threaten it against me. It's my choice each week." He doesn't nod, his eyes stay firmly on mine. "Three, it happens on my time, not yours." His teeth do that thing again, where they drag over his bottom lip.

"Are you done?"

"For now."

"Okay, so I can take you now?" He stands, goes to reach for me.

"I haven't agreed. I was just giving you examples of what I would want," I say, holding up a finger.

Whiskey-colored eyes darken, and in one swift movement he lifts me up and throws me over his shoulder. "I'll be tearing this dress off with my teeth."

I giggle.

What the ever-loving fuck.

"Put me down." I say between giggles. He does, and it's hard to wipe the smile from my face.

CHAPTER 26
WHISKEY

would have knocked the contract down by half if she had tried to push further, but luckily for me she didn't.

"I want extra time off. Eight isn't enough. I want it down to six, and you have yourself a deal," she states as I hand her the beer I carried for her when I lifted her up, we didn't get far before she demanded I put her back down.

Six months?

Will that be enough?

She puts the beer to her lips and drinks. I watch, while she knows full well I want that mouth wrapped around my cock.

"Only six months left?" I ask her.

She smiles. "Yep. If you want me." She puckers her lips. "Six months left."

Fuck, well, I didn't see that coming, thought I'd gotten away with it. But no, she always has something up her sleeve. I guess six months will work.

"I get to have you, and you can't touch anyone else," I tell her, pulling the beer from her hand.

"I agree, but neither can you."

Reaching for her leg, I turn her so the stool scrapes on the floor and she's now facing me. Leaning in, my lips inch closer to her, then she speaks.

"The contract will be done?" she asks, her eyes flicking from my lips to my eyes. She licks her lips, and I stand, reaching for her.

"Yes, the minute my hands are free, I will send her a message."

Lottie's hand stops me from grabbing her, so I pause on her thighs.

"No. Do it now."

Lifting my hands away from her gorgeous skin, I send a quick email outlining what to do, and show her then click send. Placing my cell on the counter, I reach for her again.

"No cameras?" she asks, looking around. "You don't plan to entrap me again, do you?" She smiles, but I can see there's worry behind those green eyes.

"No. I swear I'll never do that again."

"Thank you." Lottie scoots forward so I can lift

her. Her legs wrap around my waist, and she offers me a shy smile. "It's been a while."

I start walking with her in my arms. "Who was your last?"

She looks down between us when she answers, seemingly shy about her answer. "You."

Her answer takes me by surprise, but even more so, her honesty. I didn't think for a minute she'd say that.

"That makes it even better," I reply, opening the door to my room.

Lottie doesn't stop looking at me as I position her on the bed, her legs leaving my waist. Reaching for my shirt, I undo the buttons quickly and kick off my shoes one by one, pulling my belt free so my pants hang loose, then I step up to her.

"This isn't right, I don't like you," she says, shaking her head while her eyes stay locked on my body, she is trying to tell herself a lie.

Stepping closer, I reach for her dress and pull a sleeve down, her tit hangs out, and she doesn't care. Not once does she look down to cover it. I like that about her.

"You don't have to like me; you just have to fuck me."

"Well, why do you still have pants on?" she asks, standing and dropping her dress to the floor.

She stands in front of me now, naked. How the fuck did I not know she had no underwear on earlier? If I did, I wouldn't have been able to control myself, so it's probably a good thing.

Dropping my pants to the floor, I step closer and push her back, she bounces on the bed, her tits perfectly on display and needing my attention.

Bringing her legs apart, she slides her hand down to the front of her pussy.

"Do you plan to stare or touch?" she asks she flicks her hair over shoulder and the simple action pushes her tits up higher.

Goddamn, I remember her being feisty, it's one of the reasons I couldn't stop thinking about her. Plus, she tasted like the sweetest treat I've ever had.

I wanted her again and again at the time.

So, I took her over and over, as much as I could get.

"I plan to fuck, then I plan to taste. Then I plan to touch you all over."

Gripping my cock in my hand, I stroke it a few times, her eyes follow each movement while her finger slips between her folds. I can see she's glistening—wet, ready, and waiting for me.

"I'm clean," I say. "And you're on the pill?" I ask her.

She nods, her eyes transfixed on my cock in my

hand. Last time I fucked her, I had a rubber on, but this time I plan to feel every inch of her and fill her with my cum until it's leaking down her legs.

"Spread them wider, Bunny."

She does, her fingers still on her pussy, circling her clit.

"Do you want my cock in you?"

Lottie nods, biting her lips. "Words, Bunny, words. You get nothing without them."

"Will you shut up and fuck me?" she says.

Reaching down, I move her hand away, and she whimpers when I touch her between her legs. Her hips thrust upward, and it takes everything in me to not bury myself in her right there and then.

"Just one taste?" Dropping down, my tongue darts out and licks her clit. Lottie whimpers loudly and grips onto my hair. I do it again, addicted to her taste, and soon I can't stop. My finger dips into her wet pussy, and I push in hard, fucking her with my finger as I lick her clit like it's the best fucking ice cream I've ever had.

"Whiskey!" she screams.

I add another finger and feel her tighten around it, and don't slow down with my tongue. She's now thrusting with my tongue's movements and my fingers moving, I look up as my other hand reaches up and pushes on her lower stomach her head is lulled back and her tits are being cupped by her own hands, fuck, she is hot.

"I..." She attempts to speak but I slide out of her with my fingers then slide straight back in, faster, then slower, but keeping the same pace with my tongue. She goes to speak again as her orgasm hits her hard.

Pulling away, I waste no time before I slide my cock in.

She gasps, and her hands grip her hair then move down onto her flawless tits before they go back again.

Perfection.

"Too full." Lottie shakes her head, removing her hands from her hair. She reaches out and wraps her hands around my neck, sitting up. Our bodies are closer now as I grip her back and move her ass with my hands, so the rhythm never stops.

She bites my shoulder, and I feel her coming again. I stop. She whines in my ear. But I'm not ready yet. I need this to last. I need her like my next breath.

"Move, Whiskey," she says, and my name rolling off her lips forces me to start moving again.

This time I stand with her in my arms and shift her around so her back hits the wall. She doesn't let go of me as I push her against it, and fucking slam my cock in and out of her sweet pussy.

The deal she brokered was worth every bit I lost, just to have this moment.

Every fucking bit.

CHAPTER 27

Whiskey's gentle as he lies me down on the bed. My back's sore from being pushed up against the wall. He pulls out of me, and I feel his cum between my legs as it leaks out. Pushing up on my elbows, I look around the room, it's not decorated like the one at the house I'm staying at. This one, you can tell someone lives in it. On his nightstand is a picture of him and his father, their arms are around each other, and they are smiling big, next to that is a picture of just me at our wedding, in my wedding gown and the look on my face is a look of half happy half sad, I wonder if anyone else saw that look. His bed is not made, clothes lay on the floor, and not the ones we just took off either.

"Water?" he asks.

I nod as he walks out, and I eye his ass as he goes.

Then it hits me.

What the fuck did I just do?

I fucked the man I said I wouldn't ever fuck again.

Getting up from his bed, I look around his room, moving things around to make sure he isn't lying to me.

"Searching for a camera?" he asks with two bottles of water in his hands.

I pause. "And I'm meant to just trust you?"

"I guess not. You sure you don't want to check in my closet, too? Just make sure you don't have any scissors in your hands," he says, stepping closer and handing me a bottle of water. I take it from him as he steps even closer.

"Do I need to check in the closet?" I ask him.

He licks his lips and then lifts his bottle of water to them. I watch as he drinks, each mouthful as seductive as the last.

How the hell is drinking water sexy?

How does he make this sexy?

This is totally unfair.

Whiskey pulls the bottle from his lips, a bit of water still on them, and I want to lean forward and lick it off.

"There's nothing in my closet for you, Bunny, but I could get in the closet, and you could find me, we could try fucking in the dark, let's see who comes first." He puts the bottle on his nightstand behind me and takes mine from my hands, I shake my head no at his words. Twisting it open, he lifts the bottle to my lips and tips. I take a sip, and as he pulls the bottle away, he's on me again. Hands roaming me and water spilling all over the floor as the bottle drops and bounces, the contents emptying on the floor. I have to remember to breathe and remember that just because our chemistry is off the charts doesn't mean we are.

We are two people who should never work.

He's my husband.

I don't like him.

I love it when he fucks me, though. That I would do again.

Whiskey pulls us apart as he lifts me. "Tell me, Bunny… you want my cock buried deep in your pussy?" He carries me back to the bed, the same bed that's now a complete mess. He slides me down him just a touch, so I can feel him at my entrance.

"Bunny."

He hates it when I don't answer.

I look up to those amber-colored eyes and wish

it wasn't him, I wish he didn't do what he did. I now see him differently, and my trust for him is non-existent.

"Fuck me already, Whiskey."

Staying at my entrance, he kisses my breast, teasing my nipple. When he lifts up, he blows on it, making it peak even harder than it was before.

"Why are you so perfect?"

The question instantly knocks the breath out of me.

I didn't expect that from him.

I'm anything but perfect.

My father and mother have told me this my whole life. My tattoos, my style, and the way I choose to live my life has never reached their standards. I'm a complete failure in their eyes. And yet, this man who has lied and blackmailed me tells me I'm perfect. Should I believe him?

If only I could believe him.

"Shut up and fuck me, Whiskey."

"Yes, ma'am." He chuckles, spreading my legs. I'm wet, that's no surprise. But I'm also a little bit sore. He slides into me, slow and beautiful. Then he pauses, his eyes stay locked on mine, and I have to close mine so I can't see him. I can't look. I don't want to know.

There's nothing here but sex.

It's all I want from him.

Why not? He's damn good at it.

"Open your eyes, Bunny."

My eyes spring open, and when I do finally look at him, he's smirking like he knows what I'm thinking. Then he moves out and slides back in. I keep my eyes open because he needs to know he doesn't have that effect on me. This is just something to help both of our needs.

Reaching for him, I pull him down, our lips smash against each other, and his rhythm continues. Hands run up and down my naked sides until he grips my hip hard, digging his nails in, then he slams into me. Biting my lip, I swear he almost draws blood, and I stop kissing him. My head goes back, and my arms raise above my head, reaching for something to hold onto.

"That's it, rich girl, squeeze my cock." His kisses linger and tease all the way down to my breast, his mouth works my nipples like an expert. He bites, sucks, and fucks all in one marvelous go. Whiskey's hand reaches between us, and he rubs my clit with skilled precision.

The screams that leave my mouth, I can't stop, and I'm not sure I want to either.

Whiskey doesn't stop, not even when my eyes squeeze shut, and I can no longer move. He keeps going until another one builds, and soon he makes me come again. His hand leaves my clit, and he finishes inside of me.

"Bunny, this is worth every month I lost." I'm too sated to reply to that. Way too tired and sore. He pulls one more kiss from my lips before he pulls out of me and stands, then walks to his bathroom. I hear the shower start, then watch as he walks back over to where I lie on the bed. I am unable to move.

"Need a hand?" I nod my head, offering him my hand. He doesn't take it, instead he lifts me bridal style and carries me to the shower that now has steam pouring out into the bathroom. I'm too tired to argue.

Stepping in, he sets me down. My legs feel like Jell-O but I manage to stand up. He starts washing me. As the loofah moves over my arm, he pauses, his other hand dragging over my tattoos.

"Why these?"

I turn to look down at the geisha on my arm with beautifully colored roses all around her. "Roses symbolize my grandfather. He used to call my grandmother a geisha…" I pause. "As pretty as a geisha, he would say." When I look up from my arm, his movement has stopped, and he gives me a small nod.

"They are beautiful." He continues to wash me

but doesn't look up, so I eventually take the loofah from his hand.

"I can do it." And I do. I wash myself, turning so my back is facing his front and quickly wash off the suds before I'm stepping out. When I dry myself with a towel, I don't turn back to him as I head to the bedroom.

My clothes are scattered on the floor, and as I go to pick them up, his voice startles me. "I'll take you home tomorrow." Whiskey walks forward—he's still wet as I watch a single bead of water run over his taut muscles and disappear behind the towel wrapped around his waist—and takes my clothes from my hands. "I know you sleep naked, so you don't need these." Then he throws them to the floor.

Whiskey removes the towel that I'm gripping and dries himself while I stand there like a statue, unable to move. He bends, and the tanned skin shines with water droplets when he turns, show-casing me his toned back.

"If you keep staring at me like that, I'll have to fuck you again."

"That would be inappropriate," I manage to say back to him.

"Not when we're fucking. You meant out of this bedroom. What happens in it is all in my hands."

Whiskey drops his towel to the floor, his soft cock now hard again as he stands in front of me. "Are you hungry?"

My eyes drop to his cock. He chuckles, stepping forward and lifting my chin up, so I'm face to face with him again.

"Not for that, Bunny. For food."

I step forward, reaching out because I know he wants me, and I wrap my hand around his cock. "You can order, and I'll have an appetizer." Dropping to my knees, I stroke his cock, watching as the pre-cum leaves, then I lean forward, licking the top of it, making my tongue dance over his head. He breathes heavily as I take him in as far as I can go and start bobbing my head while one hand plays with his balls and the other pumps the shaft.

"Fuck, Bunny, that mouth."

I'm wet. Again.

Whiskey's hand grips my hair. Hard. Then he starts moving me faster and faster until I feel his balls tightening in my hand. "If you don't want me to come in your mouth, you better move away now." I don't move. Instead, I suck harder and faster until he fills my mouth as he continues to fuck it. He lets go of my hair and pulls me to stand.

"Now I need an appetizer." Whiskey drops, and with one strong hand he lifts my leg over his shoulder and his tongue trails a path to my clit. I fall back on the soft mattress, my hand reaches out to the nightstand, gripping it as his mouth makes delicious circles around my clit and his finger pushes in, fucking me. I'm sore, but his mouth makes me forget all about, makes me forget why I'm even doing this, and making me forget why I have this insane attraction to this man.

One hand finds his hair as my hips thrust to meet him, making him move in the direction I need him the most. His fingers pump hard and fast as his tongue shows me who's in charge. And believe me, it's not me.

I come around his finger, and he doesn't stop until I pull away. When he stands, my leg falls to the floor. "I'm hungry now."

Whiskey nods to his bed and licks his lips, me evident all over him. "Get into bed, and I'll order in." Then he walks out.

I do as he says, and when I lie down, I think of him. And what kind of situation I've just put myself in.

Was this a smart move?

My body says yes, but my head says no.

I had a plan to make this man fall in love with me.

But now, that may be harder than I had originally thought.

My phone dings, and in it is an article.

America's favorite drummer is in the hospital with two broken legs...

CHAPTER 28
WHISKEY

Walking into the room, I find her with her phone in hand and a very pissed off look on her face.

"You had his legs broken?" she screams.

Well, that was fast.

"So, you don't want fries with your order I take it?" I ask her, she screams and reaches for the photo I have of her next to my bed, it's my favorite photo, it even trumps the one of my father and me. The way she is half smiling at me in it, has my cock hard. And that dress, was worth every single penny. Fuck, I'd let her buy ten if that's what she wanted. "Don't ruin my photo!" she screams and throws it at me, still naked. I would say she looks straight out of a scary movie as she moves toward me. She crawls over the bed, naked, with her hair hanging down at her sides. Let's be honest, though. I'd still fuck her. To me, even when she's crazy, I'd still fuck her.

"His legs."

"Do you think I joke often? You should know by now that when it comes to you, I don't joke." I shrug, holding my phone in my hand. "Burger, then?" I ask, placing an order. She reaches me then, grips my phone and pulls it free from my hands.

"I should leave you. You're crazy. I liked him."

"Yeah, let's be honest, he wouldn't have waited eight months."

"Six," she corrects me holding my phone in her hand now to her naked hip.

"I need my phone to finish the order," I say, nodding to it.

"And I need you to not be so fucked up and hurt people." I reach for her face and run my fingers down her jaw.

"I don't plan to hurt you, tonight. Unless you ask." I wink at her.

Those green eyes go a crazy color as she bares her teeth at me.

"What secret stuff do you have on this phone anyway?" She pulls away and looks to my phone. The lock screen is us, at our wedding. She eyes it then looks up to me.

"For appearances, it's normal to have your wife."

"I don't have you," she bites back. She unlocks it and opens it; I watch her eyes soften just a little. "When did you take this?" she turns the phone around to the photo I know is already there.

"When you weren't snoring, just so you know."

"I don't snore."

"If you say so." I go to take the phone from her, but she is already in my messages.

"Do you message your ex?"

"Absolutely not."

"If I find out you have been texting her, her legs are to be broken too. An eye for an eye." I shrug, seems fair, really.

"Done," I tell her, nodding. She looks at me in disbelief and then goes back to searching the phone. When she is happy, she hands me the phone back.

"I hate you."

"But you would still fuck me, right?" She crawls into the bed without an answer, I order the food after leaving the room, and when it's done, I walk back in to find Lottie asleep, the sheet pulled over her lower body. She moans, and I realize she isn't snoring, but she is clearly asleep. Walking over, I pull the sheet up and over her entire body. She turns in her sleep, gripping the sheet, leaving her back bare. Leaning down, I kiss the side of her lips and slide in next to her.

When I do, she touches me, her hand finding mine, and I wrap my fingers with hers, gripping her the same way we were before I moved out. Lottie's become a sort of comfort for me, but it's snuck up unexpectedly, and I didn't want that, those nights away from her, were torture. She was a means to an end, and now all she will ever see in me is someone who blackmailed her. How could she ever love someone like me?

I don't regret what I did, and I will still go through with my plan—no matter what. But what I didn't expect is to have feelings for this woman.

This shouldn't be happening.

Closing my eyes, I grip her tight.

I don't have nightmares that night, but when I wake, she's gone.

And it's as if she were never here to begin with.

———

I walk to my car and ring Lottie, but she doesn't answer. It's no surprise. I didn't think she would after she snuck out.

Calling Barry, he answers straight away. "So, you fucked her again," he says.

"What the fuck?"

"She told Emma. I may have been listening in."

"Did she say anything good?"

Barry goes silent. "She said something along the lines of 'a means to an end,' and you 'both have needs.' And that you fucked up my favorite drummer, dude, that's not cool."

"Well," I say, smiling.

"Then, she said she still hates you, even if the sex is good," he adds.

"Hates me?" I ask him.

"Oh yeah, she then proceeded to call you a *lot* of names. None which I can repeat, of course, since I am a gentleman." He laughs then starts, "Fucker, dick head, asshole…"

"Okay, enough."

"But I'm not finished," Barry whines. "Black-mailing prick—" He stops. "Oh, hold on, that may have been Emma who said that."

"This isn't helping, Barry."

"She's at work if you're looking for her."

"Thanks."

"Whiskey…"

"Yeah…"

"What color are her eyes?"

"Green. There as vivid as a see-through lake," I answer.

"I'm sorry, man. Real sorry."

"For what?"

"That this plan of yours is going to fuck you over more so than her. Because it's you who's fallen harder." He hangs up.

I shake my head.

No. What? Just because I know the color of her eyes? No, it can't be.

I call her again.

Lottie doesn't answer.

I drive to her bar, and when I arrive, I see her smiling.

Maybe Barry is right.

Maybe that's the reason I pull away without getting out.

Maybe that's the reason I won't see her at all today.

CHAPTER 29
LOTTIE

"**L**ottie babes." My regular Dash, who I haven't seen in a few months smiles at me as he sits at my end of the bar. It's not busy yet, but it will be when the band I got to fill in for Shane's band arrive to play. Then I won't have time to breathe.

"Dash," I say, smiling, walking up to him. "Usual?" I ask.

Dash always makes me smile. I used to think he was the only decent guy out there. Maybe he still is, he and his wife have the perfect relationship and to be honest I'm a little envious.

"You know it." Dash winks as I slide his drink to him. He goes to pull out money, but I stop him.

"Nope, it's on the house."

He tips the glass bottle my way and looks around. "Hasn't changed much."

I smile, it hasn't. "Still the same, except now we're booking bands."

"Nice."

"How's Sarah?"

"Pregnant, hence why I haven't been here, and why she hasn't been with me. She is working late and meeting me after, so thought I'd kill some time and see my favorite bartender." He winks. "We are friends, right?"

"Yes." I smile.

"Sarah wanted me to invite you both over, we had read that you were married. Would you be—"

I tense at his words, and he notices and stops.

I think about it for a second or two and answer, "Sure, I'd love to."

"I could send a car; the area is a bit tricky."

"I'm sure we will be fine."

Dash smirks when I say his name.

"Whiskey?" he questions and cocks his head to the side.

"That's his name."

Dash's phone dings, he looks to it as he stands, leaving a tip on the counter, I hand him my work card.

"That's got my mobile on it, text me your address and we'd be delighted to come."

I think it's time I make Whiskey do things instead of the other way around.

———

The following day I still haven't heard from Whiskey, but then again, I haven't reached out either. I also don't intend to. I signed the contract, so it's done, I now have six months to go, and I will be free. It's a relief, and also scary, as I never wanted to be a divorcée. Not once did I see myself as that type of woman. I wanted my marriage to last forever, and with it a lifetime of happiness.

"Are you avoiding me?"

I jump and almost drop the tray of glasses in my hand. Turning around, Whiskey's standing there. I push past him and walk around the bar. It's safer with something separating us. "No, I've been working, you should know this, since you can see me." I point to the cameras.

"I'm amazed you haven't torn them down," he says.

"Oh, I thought about it." I tell him. But in truth, I need them until I figure out how to get in contact with another security company that is not my husbands.

Whiskey doesn't sit, he stands there watching me as I fidget doing everything else there is to do apart from look at him. Because if I look, I'll see him between my legs. And if I stare long enough, I will see those whiskey-colored eyes as they fuck me, but I am mad at him, not just for the cameras—for Shane too.

"You've been avoiding me. That's okay. I've been avoiding you as well."

Whiskey's answer takes me by surprise, so I look up at him. He smirks, sits, and taps the bar with his finger. "Whiskey neat."

"How ironic," I say with an eye roll as I swing around and pour him two fingers.

"I'd like you to come back with me tonight."

I slide the glass over to him, and he eyes it for a second before he looks back at me. "Is that so?"

"Yes, come home with me."

As he says it, the band walks in. One of them looks my way and winks, and when he does, my cheeks redden instantly.

"You can't fuck him, you know that, right? I'd hate to go around breaking another set of legs."

My eyes snap back to Whiskey, who has the tumbler to his lips.

"I know," I say through gritted teeth. "If you even dare do something like that again…" I fume.

"You'll what, withhold sex from me? If you do and when you cave, because we both know you will, I'll draw out you coming and watch as you scream for your release." He winks before he turns around. "If you will excuse me." He gets up, and I watch as he heads to band. I don't even bother following, instead I start wiping the bar, waiting for him to return a few minutes later. Whiskey heads straight back to the bar and sits as if he didn't go anywhere. Then he picks up his glass, and I notice his knuckles are red.

"Tell me you didn't hit him," I say, looking over at the back door then back to him.

"I didn't hit him." Relief washes over me. "I punched his fucking teeth out."

What the fuck! My eyes snap to him, and my hand covers my mouth.

"Oh, my god. Tell me you're joking. Soon I won't have any fucking bands want to perform here." I could cry. "You are ruining my life and you aren't even my real fucking husband!" I scream.

The back door flies open, and the band member that winked at me walks in holding his mouth.

"Lucky he doesn't need it to sing," Whiskey says. When I look back to him, he's smirking.

"Lottie…" I turn to my manager who's nodding for me. I look back to Whiskey as dread fills me, the band spoke to her.

"Can I have a minute?" Whiskey stands and walks to my manager before I can even reply. He says something in a hushed voice before my manager looks back at me.

"Lottie…" My manager nods for me to follow her. I look back to Whiskey who simply smirks as I leave.

"Look," she says as I sit. "What happened just before cannot happen again, I know you own this place, but I run it."

"I'll ban him."

"I was going to." Then she shakes his head. "They are high profile guests, Lottie. We can't have them mistreated. We can't risk other acts not signing up because of this."

"I'm sorry." Why am I the one apologizing, Whiskey should be.

"You've been different since him, let me close the night and you go home."

Walking out I find Whiskey already waiting at the door for me, he pulls me out the door and when it shuts behind me, he pushes me against the wall, I go to push him off, but he pushes against me.

"Bunny, Bunny, Bunny, when are you going to see that I only have eyes for you. And other eyes that dare look upon you, I will kill."

"That's like the first thing your mother teaches you—to stay away from boys holding red flags. You're a walking red flag." He leans in and as he does, he kisses my neck.

"She may have taught you to stay away from boys, but darling." He pushes against me, electing a moan from me. "I'm all fucking man and all yours."

Whiskey's hand slides down my hips and up my skirt, he pushes my panties to the side and slides a finger in, it goes in easily for him. I should be pushing him away again, but I can't seem to. We're in public, and at any time we could get caught.

"Take it." He pumps his fingers in me now, his thumb rubbing me through my panties. Then when I open my mouth, he leans in and steals my lips. Whiskey's fingers never slow and his lips claim me. I'm at his disposal to do with as he pleases. The man builds me up only to watch me crash after and I'm helpless to stop it.

My hands leave the wall and grip onto his arms,

holding him tight as he kisses me and fucks me with his fingers. When I come, he pulls out of me and pushes his body on me, our lips never breaking as his tongue slides inside my mouth. Our lips joined as one with a kiss that could light the night sky with fireworks.

It's the fall after I'm most afraid of.

Pulling away, he stays close to me, the evidence he wants me is clear in his pants as he holds me to the wall. "Come home with me tonight?"

"Okay," I say, giving in.

Whiskey pulls back, lifts his fingers to his lips, and sucks. I grow wetter just watching him.

"Tastes like my favorite drink." He touches his cock, which is hard in his pants, and he adjusts himself. "This can wait until we're home."

I can only nod as the need for him takes over me. I want that. I want my lips around it and buried deep inside me all at the same time. I'm needy for him, greedy for him.

"You better hurry up then." Whiskey reaches for my hand, and as we both turn, I see people watching us.

Shit! How much did they see?

Whiskey doesn't care, going straight to his car, and he opens the door for me.

"They saw all that, didn't they?" I ask Whiskey.

He simply smirks as he shuts the door and walks around to his side. Starting the car, he still doesn't answer me.

"You are a real asshole," I say as I reach for him, gripping his cock through his suit pants and rolling my hand up and down. "Maybe you should let me out if all you want to do is play games with everyone."

"Fuck, no." He drives faster, pushing my hand away. "That's going in you. Stop it."

I poke my bottom lip out in a full-blown pout like a schoolgirl. "You're not fair."

"Now you're catching on," he says with a smile.

I like seeing him smile.

When he stops the car, I like it even more as he wraps me around him and carries me inside his apartment.

CHAPTER 30
WHISKEY

Lottie's like an iceberg, she's too beautiful to touch for fear of the cold and too hard to crack.

But lucky for me, I have an ice pick. And I plan to use it on every inch of her.

She tears at my clothes, hands going everywhere as she wastes no time. Her hand comes into contact with my cock, and she drops down as I hold her in place. I'm still trying to get us to my room, but so far, the entrance is as far as we have gotten. Her legs are still wrapped around me. Her skirt is hiked up around her hips as she positions herself and lowers down on my length.

"Greedy, Bunny," I say, kissing those plump red lips again. She bites me back, and then starts moving fast. I stop, not even sure where I am in my apartment anymore, as I let her ride me up and down. It feels way too good to let her stop, that's for sure.

"You talk way too much," she says, her hands digging into my shoulders, her legs gripping me as she fucks me.

"I can't help myself. You make me crazy."

"Shut up! I'm almost…" Lottie moves faster as I hold her ass, helping her move. Tuning into her rhythm, I lift her and bring her back down, our bodies joining as one, and soon we're both screaming as she milks my cock with her sweet pussy. She slows her rhythm and leans in to rest her head on my shoulder. It's then I realize I'm still in the entrance of my apartment. We definitely didn't get far, so I carry her to the bedroom, the same one she snuck out of two nights ago and lie her gently on the bed. My body hovers over hers, and her smell is intoxicating and everywhere. Even on my pillows.

"You're so beautiful."

"Stop doing that," she says and pushes at me to move. I don't.

"This is an arrangement. Don't go doing this." She waves her hand from my chest to hers. "None of that is allowed. Sex is all."

"I can't tell you how beautiful you are?"

Lottie closes her eyes and throws her head back. "No. I don't want to like you, Whiskey. So, stop trying to make me." She pushes at me now, and I fall off her to the side.

"You don't want to like me. Is that a joke?" I ask her, confused.

Lottie sits up, pulling her skirt down. "No. I'd like to stay not liking you. And so far, I'm doing a great job of it."

"Fucking hell." I shake my head while removing my clothes, pulling at my torn shirt. "And they say I'm heartless."

"Oh, don't pull that act with me. Mr. I. Am. Going. To. Fuck. Up. Any. Man. That. Looks. At. You With. More. Than. A. Smile." Lottie's eyes roam my naked chest and settle on my cock, which is still hanging from my pants.

"That's one hell of a name! But honestly, do you really think that's why I did it?" I ask her.

"Yep," she answers, sounding positive.

I step back from her, putting some space between us. I was contemplating going easy on her. Maybe telling her the reasoning and ending all of this. But now, maybe not.

"Are you going to say something else?" Lottie stands, so we are face-to-face. "Want to lie to my face?"

"I like you, Lottie. Well, I did until two seconds ago."

"Two seconds ago, are you kidding?" She pushes away from me, shaking her head. "I need to go. I can't be around this toxic shit. Or around you."

"So, now you've got the time cut down, you want to run?"

"Now you've been fucked you want me to stay?" she ricochets back to me as she keeps on walking.

"Yes, fucked, you mean we had sex. That's all you're good for, right?"

She stops. Turns. Her face red and angry. "I fucking hate you, you selfish prick."

Reaching for her, I grip her wrists and pull her to me. "Do you really, though, Bunny?" I ask in a much softer tone.

The anger swarms in her green eyes as she leans in close. "Yes. Now let me go." She tries to pull free, but I don't let her. I hold her tighter and put my other arm around her back, pulling her to me, so our bodies touch. My cock's still out and is now hard because I'm touching her.

"Kiss me, Bunny."

She spits at my face and tries to pull away again, but I won't let her. Leaning forward, I take her lips in a kiss. She doesn't open. Instead, she tries to fight me. I demand her to kiss me, my lips are hard as they press against hers, but she doesn't open. Not once does she kiss me back, and when I pull back there's tears in her eyes.

Shit! I drop her arm and remove myself from her. I never want to see her cry, no matter how cruel I am to her. Never.

"I hate you, Whiskey Corton."

And I believe her.

I believe it with every part of me that, right now, she hates me.

And I hate myself even more for making her this way.

Lottie turns, her red hair a mess as she walks to the door and doesn't once look back at me.

The minute she's gone, I grab the closest thing to me and smash it to pieces.

It's ironic that it turns out it's the photograph of my father.

He's the sole reason I've targeted her to begin with.

CHAPTER 31
LOTTIE

Emma's hand soothes down my back, rubbing it to try to calm me down. I can't stay calm, though. I'm angry, upset, and want to hurt Whiskey the same way he's hurting me.

This isn't fair.

None of this is fair.

He doesn't play fair.

"Just don't have sex with him again," she says. "I'm sure he can't change the contract now."

Taking a long sip of straight vodka, which burns all the way down, I shake my head. "I don't even want to see him again. The thought of his hands on me..." I take another sip. Emma removes her hands, so I turn to face her. She's thinking. "Say it, Emma."

Her eyes look up at me, she looks guilty. "You like him… a lot."

I go to shake my head. Even though I know that's a lie. So, I don't even bother denying it. *How did my hate for this man turn into me wanting him?* I still haven't figured that part out.

"If you don't separate yourself from him, Lottie, you may just fall in love with him."

My head shakes fast. "That can't happen. I can't have that happen," I say more to myself.

But she answers me anyway. "I'm afraid it's bound to."

"How can you say that?" I stand, taking the bottle with me. I'm still in his house, and I hate that fact. I want to go back to mine. So, I walk to the closet and start packing everything, pulling it all out of the closet and into the empty suitcases and boxes I had stashed away in case I needed them.

"You don't look at anyone like you look at him."

"I look at him with hate."

She shakes her head. "No, that was there, but it's gone now. I've known you for twenty years, Lottie. I know when you truly hate something, and believe me, you don't hate Whiskey."

"I hate him."

"Do you, though?"

I turn to that voice and see him standing in the doorway. I turn away from him, continuing to pull all my stuff out and pack it. "What are you doing here, Whiskey?"

"Come to see you, Bunny."

Turning back to him, I see Emma standing. "I'm just gonna leave."

Before I can say anything to stop her, she ducks out and is gone.

"Do you really hate me, Bunny?"

"I'm trying to," I reply.

"So, no?"

I shake my head. "What do you want?" Closing that suitcase, I reach for another and continue doing the same, packing up all my stuff.

"I came to give you this." Whiskey throws some paperwork at my feet and then he turns to walk out. "The house is yours, by the way," he says as he leaves.

I look at it but don't want to touch it. The last time I touched anything with his name on it, I got fucked over into marrying him.

Once I finish packing, I ignore the paperwork that sits on the bedroom floor. Instead, I choose to finish off my bottle of vodka and allow the alcohol to do its job and numb me.

————

When I go into work the next day, the paper-work is still scattered on the floor and my head thumps from drinking way too much.

If there was one saving grace, at least I didn't fuck Whiskey last night.

Oh, that's right, I damn well did before that, though. It's what got me into this situation in the first place. Maybe I need to learn to keep my legs closed.

Mental note: *Do not, under any circumstances, spread my legs for that asshole.*

"I didn't expect to see you." Bianca my manager, walks in behind me. "Not today, anyway."

I shake my head and start setting up the bar, pulling the stools down from the tables and placing the napkins and cutlery.

"Why?"

"Your husband came back in today, booked three big bands back-to-back, all paid for. That's amazing Lottie." Her words make me stop what I'm doing.

"What?"

"Yep, so good considering the last two didn't

work out." I look to my phone, should I message him and thank him? No, I should not. It's his fault anyway.

Just as I go to slide my cell back in my pocket, it rings. Looking at the number, I don't recognize it, so I go to slide it off, but for some reason, I press accept instead.

"Lottie babes," Dash's voice rings through.

"Dash," I say, confused.

"I was calling to invite you and Corton around for dinner. You free tonight?"

"Yeah, but—"

Before I can finish, he butts in. "Good. Texting you the address now. Sarah already started cooking, so be prepared." He laughs, then adds, "Looking forward to it." Then, he hangs up.

I walk back to the bar and sigh as Clinton walks in with a giant smirk on his face.

"Clinton…" I say, confused.

"Didn't expect to see me, Lottie?" I shake my head. "I come bearing good news. Well, my version of good news anyway."

"We aren't open. It's best you leave."

"Words already out that he gave you his house." Clinton looks around, runs a finger over one of the tables. "Though, I'm not sure why."

"It's definitely time you left."

"Don't you want to hear what I have to say first, Lottie?" I hate when he says my name, it always sounds so wrong coming from his mouth. It's as if he's trying to get something from me, but he can't have it.

My cell starts buzzing, so I retrieve it and look down. It's Whiskey returning my call, so I mute it and slide the phone back into my pocket.

"Say what you came to say, then leave. I need to work."

"You know he doesn't love you, right?" I say nothing. There's no need to defend any of this, and especially not to Clinton. I have nothing left for Clinton, so I don't particularly care what he even has to say.

"How is this any of your problem, Clinton? I'm confused what your agenda is for being here."

His face goes red at my words. *Is that anger or something else?* Damned if I know.

"He's lying to you. You know that, right?"

"Goodbye, Clinton," I say, waving and walking away from him. I don't trust him, didn't when I was in a relationship with him, and don't now. Another catastrophic mistake on my part.

"Did you know your father is the reason Whiskey's father killed himself?" I stop in my tracks and turn around to face him. The bastard has a smug smirk on his face. "You didn't know," he muses. "Interesting."

"How would you know that?" I ask. My phone is incessantly buzzing in my pocket. Lifting it, I see Whiskey's name appear again.

"Ask him…" He indicates to my phone.

"No. Now leave."

Clinton shakes his head. "Surely, you can't be that silly. Can you?"

"Leave, Clinton. Now!"

He shrugs his shoulders. "I didn't take you for being a stupid girl, but I'm proved wrong."

I watch as he walks out, and when he does, I follow after him to lock the door so he can't come back inside.

———

Whiskey picks me up. I don't say hello. To be honest, I'm still processing what Clinton told me. If he's telling the truth or if he is simply stirring shit up. Whiskey and I are already fighting, and do I really need to make it worse? All my things are packed, and soon I will take them back to my old apartment.

I don't want what he says or threatens anymore. Show the world our sex tape, right now. I don't care. I give up trying to please everyone.

"You're awfully quiet," Whiskey says as he drives. I don't reply, I just stay looking out the window. "Tell me what you're mad about."

Turning to face him, I see him watching me as he comes to a stop at a red light. I can't stare long, feelings I wasn't aware of come back full force, hitting me right where it hurts. My feelings for him are growing stronger, and they scare me. I don't want to like my husband, let alone love him.

"I don't hate you, Lottie."

I turn to face him; he didn't use Bunny. He isn't watching me now, but his hands are gripped tightly around the steering wheel as he drives. Whiskey turns down a street, and soon we're pulling to the curb.

"Clinton came to visit me today."

Whiskey stops out in front of a house with a wrap-around porch. I get out, not waiting for his reply as I walk up to the house.

Dash is already there waiting, and he's smiling. "Thank god, she's been asking when you are going to arrive. We've just put the little dude to sleep, so it will be just us," Dash says, interrupting what I was going to say. I nod and offer a smile as Dash waves me in where I see Sarah, I go to introduce Dash to Whiskey when I realize they already know each other, they laugh at something, and I look at them confused.

"Work," Whiskey says.

Sarah walks over and wraps her arms around me, smiling when she pulls back. "Thank you so much for coming."

"I'm glad to get out, I'm looking forward to it."

She simply nods, and when I turn back to look for Whiskey, he's standing at the door, talking quietly to Dash.

"Unlikely friendship that one," Sarah comments. "But I guess they saw each other's demons." I look to her to see her looking at Dash in a way that shines with nothing but love. Those two are really meant to be.

"You cooked?" I ask, changing the subject.

"I did…" She pauses and looks back to the boys. "Enough chatting, let's go sit and have a drink." She links arms with me and takes me to a dining room table which is full of food and drinks. A bouquet of flowers sits in the middle.

Sarah pulls out my seat. "Come sit over here by me. We can chat and don't have to listen to their boring conversation." She smiles, and I can tell she wants to be friends. I look up at Whiskey and Dash as they walk around the table to sit across from us. Whiskey watches me with intent, waiting for something I won't and can't give him.

"So, how's it all been since the wedding?" Sarah asks, pouring herself a drink.

When no one answers, she looks around at us and stops when she sees the look on her husband's face. "Okay, how about a drink then?"

"The marriage has been shit. What about yours?" I ask her, smiling.

She looks taken aback, but plays it off as she answers, "Good. Dash and I..." She looks up at him, and he looks back with love shining in his eyes. "We're really good."

"You must be one of the lucky ones." I lift the drink she just poured for me and take a sip of it, then turn to see Whiskey's still staring at me.

"Well, you must be happy he ended the contract then," Dash says.

The wine in my glass spills all over my skirt at the shock, then I look up to Whiskey, wanting answers. "What is he talking about?"

"You didn't read the paperwork," he says, stating the obvious. "Of course you didn't."

"Excuse me, but the last time you gave me something with paper involved, it ruined my life," I reply.

"That's how you see me? Ruining your life?" he asks, his temper escalating.

"Tell me, Whiskey, how else am I meant to see you? Or am I just meant to focus on the great sex and not the life part, you know, where that's ruined for me."

Whiskey pushes back from the table. He goes to speak but shakes his head. "I tried to make up for that. I've tried to compensate you."

I stand, my hands slamming on the table. "You gave me a house."

"What!" Dash says, his eyes swinging from me to Whiskey.

"He did. He thinks I want to live in that place by myself, no I want to go back to my old life, with my friend." I tell him.

"Well, you can." He says pushing the seat back to it falls to the ground.

"I'm sorry," I tell them. "I didn't think…" I get up and follow him out. This did not go as planned —at all.

CHAPTER 32
WHISKEY

"You gave her your house?" Dash asks, shocked.

"I was thinking of her."

"Oh, my god. You love her." Sarah's hand goes over her mouth.

"No, I don't." Do I? No. That can't be right. "I have to go. I need to take Lottie home, or she might think she can walk. I wouldn't put it past her." I head outside and see her waiting by the car. Her back's against it as she plays on her cell phone. I hit the unlock button making her turn around.

"I'm ordering an Uber."

"Get in the car."

"Whatever."

I get in, waiting for her. She opens the door and slides in quickly, which surprises me, but she turns away immediately so she's looking out the window.

"You should be happy. You're getting what you want."

"I didn't want any of this. What is so hard for you to understand about all this?"

"I know that. But I have done as much as I can to make this not so hard on you. And you're still a bitch."

"Fuck you, Whiskey!" She turns to face me, and when I look to her, her face is smug as she smiles. "Why don't you tell me the real reason you did this? Tell me, Whiskey. Tell me the real goddamn reason."

I pull over on the side of the road. We aren't close to home, but I can't drive and have this conversation with her. "What did he say?" I ask, referring to Clinton.

"I want to hear it from your lips, Whiskey. I deserve that. I deserve to know why you chose me."

"You really want to know?" I ask her.

"Yes. Tell me."

"I hate your father with a passion. I was planning on making him hurt the same way I did. I wanted to destroy him."

Lottie's mouth opens, then closes, then opens

again. "Why?" she asks, shocked.

"He killed my father, and he was the bastard who was fucking my mother."

"You said he committed suicide, my father loves my mother, he would never."

"He did, because of what your father did."

Lottie appears confused at first. "What did he do?" she asks.

I look away. I don't know if I want to tell her that part of the story but decide she has to know. "The affair gave her hope, she left my father for him."

"No. My father would never do that. That would ruin his precious image."

"He did. She even fell pregnant."

"No," she says, shaking her head. "I'm an only child."

"You are…" I pause, not wanting to tell her this part. "The child died after birth."

"You're lying. Why? Is that all you do?" she screams.

"Ring him. Ask him."

"What did I have to do with anything?" she asks with her phone now clutched in her hand.

"I wanted to take away what's most precious to him, and that is you." She shakes her head and gets out of the car. I wait and watch as she puts her cell to her ear. Her eyes close, and I get out, tears start leaving her eyes as I walk around to her.

"Is it true?" she whispers.

I can't hear his reply.

It starts raining, tiny droplets of water touch her face and she doesn't even bother to wipe them away as she waits.

"He told me. He told me, Father." She turns to look at me. Her green eyes big and red. "You had a child with another woman?" Her eyes don't leave mine. "Do you know you caused a man to kill himself?" she questions, then she pulls the cell away from her ear and I hear every word he said.

"Lottie, I don't have time for this, but if you must know it was a long time ago, and I was hurting. Your mother and I were going through a rough patch, and I needed someone to lean on. Be reasonable. Your mother knows and she forgave me. Now I need you to do the same. We can't have this kind of issue hanging over our heads." She doesn't reply, she simply hangs up on him looking to me.

"You got what you wanted. Me to hate my father. Congratulations, it worked. Now take me home so I never have to see either of you again." Lottie goes to step off, and I step in front her, my body blocking hers.

"Don't do this."

"Do what?" she asks angrily. "Hate you?" She leans in closer to me. "Too late. I used to hate you. Now?" She shakes her head. "Now, I despise you."

I reach up and touch her face. "You don't, you're just angry."

She pushes my hand away like it's burning her. "Don't fucking touch me. The contract is done, is it not?"

I nod, and she sighs.

"Good. I don't want to see you ever again. Take your fucking house back and get out of my life." She turns to start walking. Cars fly by us on the busy road as the rain becomes heavier.

"Get in the car, Lottie, before you get hurt."

"Lottie..." she mimics. "Great! Now I'm Lottie."

"Bunny."

She flips me off as she keeps walking. Following her, I step up behind her and grab her wrist. She pulls to get free.

"Get in the damn car, and I won't bother you again."

"You promise?"

I feel defeated, but I tell her the truth. "I promise."

Lottie turns, walking back to the car.

I'm not sure what I did was the right thing. I wanted vengeance for my father, vengeance on a man who didn't take into consideration anyone's feelings but his own. He ruined my family and destroyed my father in the process. My father died of a broken heart.

I was hoping to never be the same way.

But as I watch her get in the car, I realize my mistake.

I didn't expect *her*.

Lottie Corton.

I guess I'm more like my mother than I thought —falling for a member of the Snow family. It killed one of us, hopefully it doesn't kill me, too.

CHAPTER 33
LOTTIE

Lies, everything is built on lies. I'm so angry it's best I keep my mouth shut and not say a word as he drives. Every time I look in his direction, he's gripping the wheel so hard I'm afraid it will break. When he comes to a stop out front of his house, I straighten up.

"This isn't my home."

"It is. Read the paperwork, Lottie."

I turn to face him, and he doesn't even look my way. It's probably for the better that he doesn't. I get out, slam the door, and fast walk to the door. I don't even want to walk into this place. I want to go far away from everything that represents Whiskey Corton.

Turning around, I watch as his car drives off, leaving me standing out front. I never thought this would be where my life would take me. I had dreams. And none of this was included. I feel almost ripped off. How is this fair?

Walking in, I shut the door behind me and head to the bedroom. Picking up the paperwork from the floor, I start to read it over.

He's ended the contract.

Like he said, all deals are off, and in the folder, I will find the only copy of the evidence regarding that night. I reach for it and snap the disk in half, then again into smaller pieces. Somehow, that gives me some gratification, but it's small and doesn't last for long.

The contract has ended, but he's also left the deeds to this house, which is now in my name. But I don't want it.

Pushing away the paperwork like it's burning me, I walk straight out of the bedroom and into the kitchen. Picking up a bottle of vodka, I open it. His house, or should I say my house, is stocked full of booze.

Before I can drink the first sip, the doorbell rings. I know it's not him, so I wonder if I should even open it. It rings again, then there's constant banging on the door. Gripping the bottle in one hand I walk over, pulling it open. My father's standing there, a look of worry and anger written all over his face. He goes to speak, and before I can hear a word that leaves his lying mouth, I shut the door in his face.

"Lottie," he yells, and just as I go to walk away the front door opens.

Shit! Why didn't I lock it?

Father steps into the doorway, so I can't close it. "You shut the door in my face?" he asks, clearly angry.

"You deserve that and a whole lot more," I spit back at him, taking another drink from my vodka bottle.

"This is what's become of you?" He nods to the bottle in hand. "You drink now?"

"I always drank. But you've never stopped for one minute to take notice of me," I say with an eye roll. "Oh, that's right... I was never marrying the right man or looking the part you desperately wanted me to play."

"Lottie..."

I hold my hand up and shake my head. "If you're going to spew your lies at me, you better make them good. Otherwise, this vodka will end up all over you."

"Where's your husband?"

I laugh at him. "You mean my fake husband?" He looks at me, confusion plastered all over his face. "Carry on, you don't have long, my patience has already gone."

"You were never meant to find out."

"No, I believe if I hadn't found out you would have never told me, am I right?" I spit that last bit right back at him and take another big mouthful of vodka.

"Will you just put the damn vodka down so we can talk?"

I shake my head. "Carry on… with your lies."

"So, you're just going to take his word for it? Over your own father?"

I scoff at him. "You pretty much admitted it to me on the phone, Father. Who do you think I am?" I ask, shaking my head. "You need to leave. I have to pack up and move. And you being here isn't helping or getting it done quicker."

"Why are you moving?"

"Why did you have an affair?"

"Your mother left me. I met Katrina, and it was instant. I loved her. We even planned on keeping the baby. I was going to tell you, but it all happened so fast. The baby died. Katrina fell apart. And then your mother asked me to come back, so I did. It was good for my business to be seen as a family man."

As he finishes talking, the door flings open, and

Whiskey walks in with my purse in his hand. He pauses, and when he sees my father, both of them straighten their backs.

Another mental note: *Lock the damn door.*

"Gerald," Whiskey says with anger seething from the single word.

"What's going on with you and my daughter?"

Whiskey's eyes flick to me.

I lift the bottle of vodka, nodding to him, then take another sip, "I will not be around you when I'm drunk, Whiskey, you may record me again." It's going to my head, and I'm well on my way to being drunk.

"She was a very sweet form of revenge," he says, his eyes leaving mine to look to my father.

"Revenge?"

"You ruined my life. Ruined my family's life and killed my father."

My father doesn't even flinch. "Your father did that to himself."

"He came to see you before it happened."

"He did," my father replies. "And I will tell you the same thing I told him. I loved your mother, but sometimes love isn't enough."

Whiskey's eyes flick to me.

"Yeah, love is never enough," I muse.

"Lies," Whiskey says back to me.

"Why is she saying this marriage is fake?" my father asks.

"I blackmailed her into marrying me so I could take your most prized possession and ruin it like you ruined mine."

I gasp at his words.

Father takes a step forward to me. "You black-mailed my daughter?"

"You should leave, Gerald."

"No. I want to know what you did to her and how this will effect me."

"He taped me having sex with him," I say as I wave the bottle of vodka. "While I was tipsy, or drunk, not sure which anymore."

Whiskey didn't think I would say it, but honestly, my care factor has gone.

Completely.

Out the window with any semblance of self-respect that I had with it.

"You what," my father screams, turning his angry eyes to Whiskey who is staring at me.

I shrug, watching the two of them, lifting the bottle to my lips to cover my smirk.

"This is what you blackmailed her with to marry you?"

"Don't act like you care, Father. I know you

don't. I destroyed the evidence today. You are fine," I say with an eye roll.

He turns to face me, his hand running through his hair. "Of course I care, Lottie. I've always been the one to care. To take care of you, make sure you have everything you need. And this is how you repay me?"

My back hits the wall, dizziness taking over me. "You're a superb liar." I take another sip from the vodka bottle.

"You've had enough, don't you think?" Whiskey says.

"You can leave now," I wave Whiskey off, then look to my father. "You can leave too."

"I love you, Lottie," my father says.

I harrumph at him, not believing one word that man says. "The only thing you love in this life, Father, is your stupid reputation, which is what got me into this position in the first place," I say to him as a hiccup leaves my mouth.

"You could have come to me instead of marrying him," he seethes.

"Yes, because you're the easiest person to talk with. Father, I have to make appointments to see you," I reply. "Does Mother know you fucked Whiskey's mother?" His eyebrows raise at me.

"Yes. Yes, she knows." He wipes his brow. "It's why she never approved of your marriage."

Oh, well that makes sense. I just figured it was Mother being a bitch. But she never liked Whiskey due to who his parents are.

"It's not Whiskey's fault you couldn't keep your dick in your pants and had to fuck his mother, ruining his life."

Whiskey smirks.

I give him a pointed look as I speak to him next. "But it is your fault that you fucked me over. I had nothing to do with any of this. You came in and ruined my life. You turned it upside down and made me have feelings for a man I will never trust."

"You can trust me, Lottie." I shake my head, pushing myself up and off the wall. The bottle slips from my grip and shatters at my bare feet.

"Lottie, you're a mess," my father says.

"You made me this way. Now *leave.* I need to go to bed." I step off, and before I realize what I'm doing, my feet are cut by the broken glass. It stings, and I drop, but before I hit the floor, Whiskey's there, lifting me into his arms. My head spins and I clutch it.

"You should go," Whiskey says to my father.

"She needs me," my father replies.

"No, she doesn't. Now leave my hous—"

"My house," I interject.

"Yeah, yeah, Bunny," he says into my ear.

"I'll call tomorrow, Lottie." I don't even bother replying to him as Whiskey carries me to the bedroom. I don't hold on, but he doesn't need me to. He's strong enough to hold me himself.

"I am sorry. So sorry," Whiskey says.

"Your words won't work. Actions now, that's all you have left."

Whiskey looks at me, and I look back at him. When he walks in the bedroom, he places me on the bed and kisses my forehead. It's soft, and he lingers, breathing me in. "If that's what it takes."

"It will take more than that," I say, my head falling back until I am lying flat on the bed. Whiskey disappears and comes back with a first aid kit and sits down, lifting my foot, then gets to work on it.

"Why are your things packed?" he asks.

"I was moving out."

"Where to?"

"Back to my old place. I don't want to be here a second longer, there are too many memories here and they are all bad."

"Do you want to move in with me?" he asks.

"No," I answer without hesitation.

"The offer is always there."

"Was I just a way to get to him?"

"Yes." I close my eyes at his words, trying not to let them hurt me. "That is, until you weren't."

"I still hate you," I say.

Whiskey's hand rubs my leg, and it takes everything in me to not climb over him. I want him. I've never denied that there's an attraction to him, even when I didn't like him, I was attracted to him.

"That's okay, we have time."

"I want a divorce." His hand pauses, then it moves again. "I also want you to kiss me."

Whiskey stops, putting my foot gently down on the bed and turns around. My eyes open as I watch him come closer, his body hovering to the side of me.

It may be the alcohol that makes me see things, but the way he's looking at me, it scares me. Whiskey's staring at me the way you do at someone you love. As if he only has eyes for me. He hasn't always looked at me like that. When did that change? How did this change?

"You're looking at me weird," I say to him.

"It's because I'm seeing you differently, and I'm sorry it's taken me this long."

Before I can change my mind or push him away, his lips touch mine ever so softly. It's as if I will break any second. A tear slips free from my eye, and I don't understand why. But he doesn't stop, his lips apply more pressure as they claim mine. His soft lips move, and in doing so, I open my mouth for him as he claims my tongue. He's gentle, soft, caring, and it's not like we haven't kissed before. No, this is more cautious, as if he's worried this will be our last kiss. It just may be, but I'm not ready to stop him yet.

His hands touch my face, cupping it, as he looks into my eyes.

Will this be our last kiss?

I don't push him away. His lips are like a beautifully toxic thing, you want it, but you know you shouldn't. I can feel something in my chest hurt, like a pain I can't quite describe.

Whiskey is nothing I wanted, but everything I need.

I can't lie to my drunken self any longer.

My feelings for Whiskey are there, even when I want to hide them and run away from them. They are there and they are full force.

Pushing him away, he stays above me, his lips wet and red from our kiss.

"You should go," I manage to say.

"I can stay."

My head shakes before my mouth can say yes.

"I don't want to go," he says, leaning down, touching my lips with another soft kiss. "But I will." He pushes up, and when he stands, he straightens his shirt and looks down on me. "You are the most beautiful woman I have ever seen. It's one of the reasons I could do what I did. Because I wanted you. There was never any question about that." Whiskey turns and walks out, leaving me drunk and aroused as I lie on the bed, confused by his words.

CHAPTER 34
WHISKEY

I send her a message the following day, she doesn't reply. When I go to the house, she isn't there, and neither are her things.

I give her another day before I head to her work.

When I go there, the manager tells me she hasn't been in at all or notified them why. She shrugs her shoulders before she walks off.

Calling her cell, it doesn't even ring. Simply goes straight to voicemail.

"Hey, it's Lottie. I can't answer the phone right now. I'm too busy living my best life in Paris." Then it goes blank.

Heading to where she used to live with Emma, I bang on the door and the person who answers it, I don't expect.

"Man, what are you doing here?" Barry says, rubbing his face as if he's just woken up.

"Where is she?" I ask, looking behind him.

Barry opens the door wider, and I don't see her things. "You mean Lottie?" I nod. "She stopped by this morning to say goodbye. I assumed you were going with her."

"Where?"

"Paris. She went to Paris." I look at him, confused. "She said she needed to breathe, and Paris helps her do that."

"Fuck."

"Hey, asshole." Emma walks up behind Barry, wrapping her arms around him. "You really fucked her up. She's a mess."

"Where is she?"

Emma looks away from me but answers, "Do you even want her?"

"Yes, I want her."

"Why?"

"Because I fucking love her," I say, and shock myself as those words leave my mouth.

"Go to the Eiffel Tower at seven. She said she will ring me then, telling me she's there, as she wants to watch the lights."

"That's in France," I say, shocked.

Emma looks at me and gives me a pointed look.

"Well, you better hurry, then." She steps back with a smiling Barry as she shuts the door in my face.

Fuck! Paris.

Really?

I hate that place.

———

The last time I was here was with my mother. It was the last time I remember her happy. It's mid-September and the weather's nice, so I make my way to the tower and look around. There are many places she could be. Tourists line up everywhere to watch the tower as it shines bright. It really is a magnificent sight.

People come up to me asking me to buy shit. I ignore them and keep walking. I will find her. Tourists bump into me, as they're too busy gazing upward instead of watching where they are going.

"Whiskey?"

That voice stops me. I turn around to see Lottie standing behind me.

She gives me a puzzled look, then glances around, confused. "Is that you?"

I walk up to her, and in two seconds I have her face in my hands and my lips on her mouth. She doesn't kiss me back at first, but eventually she does. Her hands touch my arms, and she sinks into me. How I love her touch. Then, all of a sudden, she pulls back and looks at me.

"What…" She shakes her head.

"I came for you."

"This isn't some movie, Whiskey, where flying across the world and coming to tell me you love me will make this all better."

"How did you know what I came to say?"

Lottie's mouth opens and closes. "I was joking." She rubs her arms and looks at me nervously.

"Should we go eat?" I ask.

She nods and I reach for her hand, but she pulls it away before I can capture it with mine. Waving a cab down, we slide in, and she directs him where to go, and soon we're pulling up in front of a café called Angelina's. Neither of us speak in the cab, but I can feel her watching me. I must admit I didn't think this through.

The realization that I love this woman only happened a short time ago, and now that I know it, I don't plan to lose her, no matter what. And I will do everything in my power to make sure she knows it.

She gets out of the cab, and I follow her inside.

The waiter seats us, and Lottie orders a chocolate crepe and a coffee for me and tea for her.

"Do you want food?" she asks.

"No."

The waiter leaves, and we sit in Angelina's in an awkward silence. One thing I never liked about Paris is how close all the tables are to each other. There's no privacy at all.

"Why are you here, Whiskey?"

"You guessed it earlier."

"Say it, Whiskey. It's not real if you don't speak the words," she says as our drinks are placed in front of us.

"I love you, Lottie Corton. Is that what you want to hear?"

She stirs her tea, looking down at it.

"And I'm sorry. I'm sorry it took so long for me to realize it. Sorry for what I did, and that's how our story started. I'm sorry."

She looks up at me with wet eyes. "I'm highly emotional." She lifts her drink and takes a sip. "I'm also pregnant," she says, making me push my chair back to a stand. I look down at her, and her eyes fall to the teacup, not looking at me.

The waiter comes back over and hands her a chocolate crepe. She thanks him and starts eating. "I've been craving them."

"You were drunk," I tell her, reminding her of the other night, was she drinking when she knew?

"I didn't know then," she says, defending herself. "It was the next morning when I couldn't stop throwing up. Then I realized I was late. I haven't told a soul, you're the first. I even waited until I got here to take the test, what better way to find out you are going to be a parent then the city of love."

I sit back down.

Eyes that were on me are no longer there.

"So, you came to Paris?" I ask her, confused.

"I needed to breathe, and what better place to do that than in Paris, I mean, I have a rich husband, so I booked it with his card, business class of course."

"You flew around the world to decide to breathe?"

Lottie takes another bite and looks up, watching me with those sea green eyes that have me trapped, in her. So many emotions run through me. Like how the fuck did this happen? But I already know how, don't I? And I don't know if I'm angry, excited, scared, or all three at the same time.

"I needed to know I could do this." She looks down at her stomach. "And I needed to be as far away from you and my father as possible."

"That didn't turn out quite like you expected."

She nods. "Yep, but I guess life has a way of sneaking up on you, hey?" she says, looking at me.

"I never wanted to be a father," I tell her.

Lottie doesn't look at me. She's also not shocked by my admittance. She just waits to see what else I have to say.

"I never wanted to be married again, either."

Her breathing picks up. "What a way to tell your wife, in Paris, that you don't want her," she says. "You know how to make my heart pitter-patter, don't you?"

I reach forward and take her hand in mine. "What I am saying is, Bunny, I never wanted any of that"—I pause, looking right at her—"until I met you."

She pulls her hands away from me. "You can't do that. You can't come here and try to make me love you. It doesn't work like that. You didn't just fuck up, you ruined me, Whiskey." A stray tear leaves her eye, I reach for her wanting it gone. She shouldn't be the one breaking. It was me who fucked this up.

"And I would do it all again, if the end result was that I got to have you."

Lottie's hands come to the top of the table, and she clasps them together. "But you don't have me."

"No, but I want you. And I will do whatever it is you need for me to do to show you. I know words won't help, but maybe showing you will?"

"I want to go to Disneyland Paris," she says, changing the subject.

"Disneyland is where I will take you then."

She stands, and when she does, she covers her mouth. I rush to her, my hand on her stomach and my other on her back, rubbing it slowly.

"Are you okay? Should we go to the doctor?"

She manages to take a deep breath. "No, it's just the sickness. It's really hitting me. I should probably go to the doctor when I get home."

I step back. "You haven't been?" I ask her.

She shakes her head. "I took a test. It said it reads as early as two weeks."

"You need to go to a doctor."

Lottie waves me off. "I will when I'm home."

I pull out my cell, and her hand stops me. "Don't try to find me a doctor. I've told you already when I'm home I will deal with it."

"Do you plan to keep it?"

She slips the money inside the folder to pay the bill, and I immediately give her the money back and put mine inside instead.

"I can pay for myself." Lottie shakes her head as she starts walking to leave. "And I haven't decided.

A baby is a big deal." The night air hits us when we exit the café. "Do you want me to keep it?"

"It's you, so yes."

She nods, and we come to a standstill. Both of us just standing there staring at each other. "I am sorry about your father and your mother."

"I'm learning I shouldn't hold grudges."

She smiles. It's soft but I'm pretty sure it's also forced.

"Especially if this baby's grandfather is going to be related to you. Family dinners could be awkward."

"I may never like the man, but I will give him the respect that's due for you."

"You talk as if you will be in my life."

"Baby or no baby, I want you either way."

She turns and looks down the street, then back to me. "Meet me tomorrow. You can take me on a date to Disneyland." Then she gets in a cab, and it drives away.

Disneyland?

What the fuck?

CHAPTER 35
LOTTIE

Whiskey messaged me all night. A string of messages I didn't reply to.

> Whiskey: It's because you make me smile when I didn't know I needed to.

> Whiskey: When you smile, my heart does this stupid pitter-patter I didn't agree to.

> Whiskey: I didn't love you straight away, I just knew I wanted you.

> Whiskey: I'd give it all up for you. I want you to know that.

> Whiskey: And I'd still break any mans' arms or legs if they even think they can take you from me.

A black car pulls up outside my hotel. I told him where I was staying this morning, not commenting on the messages. Whiskey gets out, opens the back door to let me in, then walks around to the other side and slides in beside me. The driver pulls out and I smile, seeing what he has on—sneakers, black jeans, and a white T-shirt.

"You look good."

His hand rests between us and his fingers are almost touching mine.

"I slept way better."

"No sickness?" he asks.

I shake my head. "Is this what it's going to be like now?" I indicate between us. "I don't know you as this person. Stop trying to tread lightly around me, Whiskey. I liked who you were, apart from the blackmailing, stop with the small talk." He reaches for my hand, then takes it and squeezes it.

"I'd take you because I want you. You want me like that?"

I smirk. "I like you like that."

Whiskey leans over and kisses my lips. I don't know if it's the news that I'm pregnant or what, but I want those lips on me. I like those lips all over me.

I ask him questions—he answers without hesitation. He tells me more about his mother. How she was beautiful but ultimately how broken she was, and that his father had a big role in raising him until he gave up on life. How the business is now that he's running it, and how it was crumbling when he took it over. Now it's a billion-dollar business. Hearing him say those words shock me.

"Do we have a prenup?" I ask him.

"No. I knew I didn't need one with you."

"That's a lot of trust in someone you've pissed off. I could have taken you for everything."

"You aren't that kind of person. Plus…" He smirks. "I have excellent lawyers."

I walk into the park. It's so beautiful, a way to break up the chaos of my life right now. The smell of funnel cakes, crepes and fresh air have a way of cleansing the soul, and that's what we're here to do. We need this fresh start.

Whiskey comes around and slides his hand in mine. "I like seeing that."

I turn to him, and he's nodding his head at my smile. "I like to smile if the moment deserves it."

"I like being the one to put it there."

"Technically, it was a man named Walt, but sure, if you want to try to claim some of that, go ahead," I say with an eye roll as we walk toward the gates.

"I'll claim as many as I can."

Whiskey pays for our tickets, and soon we're walking in. There's a street parade, and it takes me back to my childhood. Disney is a huge piece of my life. I even have tattoos on my body of Disney characters.

"I'll take you to every Disneyland in the world if this is the way you'll smile at me," he says.

Later on in the day, as I get another chocolate crepe—I really am going to miss these things—he leans in and kisses the side of my lips and licks.

"I'm just tasting."

I smirk. My heart beats hard, and I wonder where along the way I fell in love with Whiskey.

Was it when we slept together again?

Or was it our last kiss?

All I know is when he touches me, I'm deliriously happy. Butterflies take off in my belly, and I wonder how they will ever calm down.

———

Whiskey's moved me to his hotel room—all my things are here. I've noticed he likes to do that, move me around to his liking.

At first, I thought it was annoying, but now I kind of like it. I like the way he stares at me when he thinks I'm not looking. The way he grabs my hand when I'm not paying attention.

He's done a lot of wrongs to me, and my trust for him will have to be built and earned. But when I lie on his stomach, I see those whiskey-colored eyes and smile.

"It's not going to be easy."

"Nothing good ever comes easy."

"There's going to be days I will hate you."

"I can handle whatever you throw at me," is all he replies.

"Even if it's just me?" I ask him, wanting to know how he feels.

He brushes a hair from my face. "Definitely, if it's just you."

I rest my head on his chest. His fingers keep brushing through my red hair. My hands touch his sides, and I slide up his shirt until they touch his bare skin.

"Bunny."

I smile on his chest.

Whiskey reaches under my arms and pulls me

up, sliding me until our faces are close. "Do you know what you're doing?"

I bite my lip. "You are my husband, are you not?"

"I am," he answers, his eyes growing dark.

"Well, I just want to touch my husband, that's all."

He puts his hands to his sides. "Touch away." He smirks as I lift his shirt and then straddle him. My hands roam up and down his tanned skin, feeling the ripples underneath my fingers.

"When do you work out?" I ask.

"Every morning. I became addicted after my father died. It was my outlet, but a little fiery red head ruined that for me on a workout bench, now when I look at it, I see her naked."

I move back on his body, feeling him harden underneath me.

"We can always do it again, in the gym." I tug at his top "I think this is unfair. One of us has our top off while the other doesn't."

"Does this feel weird?" I ask him, my hand coming to a stop.

"What?"

"Us," I answer truthfully.

"No. It feels like the most natural thing I've ever done," he says it with so much confidence it's hard not to believe him. I wonder if I will feel the same way some day. His hand touches my face. "It's fine for you to have doubts. You'd be silly to trust me. And you aren't a silly girl, just a girl who does things for those she loves."

"It's going to take time," I say, defending myself.

"Time is fine. Time I can give."

I lean down and kiss him; he takes charge and wraps me in his arms as my body falls onto him. Soon we become all hands and mouths, touching, and kissing everywhere. My pants end up on the floor, and so do his.

I push him down and climb onto his lap. "Time is all I can give," I say as I lower myself onto him. My head drops back, and his hands grab each breast, gently squeezing them, pinching the nipple before I start to move.

"Fuck, you're beautiful."

There is that word again—not once have I felt ugly around him. He always tells me how beautiful I am, and it just eggs me on even more as I move my hips back and forth, my clit rubbing with the friction.

Whiskey slaps my ass and grips my hip, helping me move even faster. I lean forward, our lips smashing together, while my hips don't stop moving. They can't stop moving because I can feel it coming. I can feel that any second he is about to take me to heaven, but this time when I come back, I won't be falling down to hell.

No, this time, I'm sure he will catch me.

———

We spend one more day in France before we head home. I slept the whole plane ride home, and he didn't even proposition me for the Mile High Club. Even though I would have loved it too. When we arrive home, my father is standing at our door. Whiskey asked that I move into the apartment with him, but we popped past the house to see if there's anything we need. My father stands from sitting on a step as my mother hovers around him. My mother turns to face me. Her nose turns up in disgust at Whiskey holding my hip protectively.

"You're still with him? Even after what he did?" she asks.

For a change, my father doesn't interject.

"You're still with him even though *he* had a kid with someone else?"

She gasps at my words. "That is irrelevant.

This"—she waves between Whiskey and me—"is wrong. And he will only use you."

I've definitely thought of that, but hearing it come out of her mouth doesn't make me feel any better either. However, Mother doesn't know him like I do.

"Let's hope you are wrong, Mother," I say, walking up to them.

When I stand in front of them, I look at my father who still hasn't said a word. "Why are you here?"

"You weren't answering. We were worried and took a chance you might be here," my father finally says.

"Now you're worried? Or are you here to see what else you can get out of Whiskey for your…" I use air quotes, "… charities," I say, dropping my hands.

"No. I want nothing from him," he says, eyeing Whiskey then looking back to me. "Apart from you getting as far away from him as possible."

"He loves me, do you know that?" I say to both of them. My hand covers my mouth as I feel my sickness coming on again. It takes no prisoners and comes on at any time during the day. Who on earth called it morning sickness? It should be all day sickness.

"See, he makes you sick, even your body is telling you that."

Whiskey steps forward and starts rubbing my back. He's booked me in to see the doctor tomorrow, and I'm hoping the doctor can give me something for this. When the wave passes, I stand back up and wipe my mouth with the back of my hand. Whiskey hands me a bottle of water, and I take it greedily.

"Oh, my god." My mother's hand flies to her mouth, and my father looks at her, confused. I know she's just figured it out by the look in her eyes.

"You should leave. Lottie needs to rest."

My father looks to him with hard eyes.

"You're pregnant?" my mother asks.

I neither confirm nor deny.

My father looks between Whiskey and me, confused. "You slept with him even knowing he taped and blackmailed you?" he asks, confusion knitting his brows.

"Yes." I know it sounds dumb. But he's a weakness of mine. And a man I am falling in love with. Hard and fast.

"Did you intend to tell me?" my mother asks, her hands going to her hips.

"Yes, after the doctor visit tomorrow," I say.

Whiskey pushes me toward the door. "If you'll excuse us, she needs to sleep."

My mother scoffs but lets us walk away.

My father's hand lands on Whiskey's shoulder, halting him. "You look after her. I mean it. That shit you pulled to get her isn't acceptable." I look to him confused. I haven't seen this side of him, sure in the fake version of it when he is pleasing people. But I can always tell when he is fake, this seems real. Like he might actually care. Is that even possible?

"I will," is all Whiskey replies, then pushes me along. Once we're inside, he lifts me up and carries me to our old bed, laying me on it.

"I didn't know they were going to be here," I tell him once the front door is shut.

"I know. I told them."

Well, that takes me by surprise, but I don't comment on it.

We aren't meant to be staying here, but he climbs in behind me anyway, pulling the covers over us and rubs my back until I pass out.

And when I dream with my hand in his, I dream of him.

CHAPTER 36
WHISKEY

"**M**aybe I will move back into my apartment with Emma," she says the next day as her leg bounces at the doctor's office. We went for a blood test earlier and now we are here to find out the results. I would like to say I've been giving her space, but it's impossible. How do you give someone space when its them you want. And I know she wants me, even if she hates the fact that she does.

She pulls away. Then comes straight back. Exactly like she is doing now.

"Is that what you want?" I ask her.

"Stop grinding your jaw." She says those eyes coming to fall on me. "I mean, we never really had a proper beginning, it's natural to want that, right?"

"Our beginning is something no other will have." I tell her.

"Yeah, blackmail." She pulls her hand away and I reach for it and pull it straight back.

"No, at first. I didn't intend to blackmail you. It took time. But when I saw the opportunity, I knew I couldn't resist. We fucked in my gym, which has recordings."

"Why don't you live in that house anymore?" she asks.

"It was a rental, I had it for a few years but decided it was best to go back to mine." The doctor calls our name, and we both stand, gripping her hand which is sweating. I don't let go as we walk to the door and into the office. The doctor nods to me, he and I have worked together before.

"It's good to see you Whiskey, I had heard you got married. This is a pleasant surprise." He waves to Lottie, whose leg is shaking.

"It is, very pleasant." He nods and turns to his computer.

"I suppose you would like the results from the labs collected?" we both nod at the same time, and I even think at one stage I squeeze her hand a little too hard as she gives it a tug.

"Yes," I manage to say.

"Well, congrats, you are both to be parents. I

want to get you in for an ultrasound so we can figure out how far along you are."

"Early." Lottie says, and I see a tear roll down her cheek.

"Are you happy?" I ask her, the doctor hands us some forms and we thank him as we leave.

"I…" she shakes her head, her red hair falling into her face.

"It's unexpected, that's for sure." I tell her.

"Yes." She nods her head. "I want to move back," she says. "I need more time; this is all a lot. And you are a lot, we have great chemistry, and I'm pretty sure I'm falling in love with you, but I need time."

"Time." I nod.

"Yes. You need to give me that, you have this thing with not giving me choices. You need to give me choices Whiskey."

"I'm used to getting what I want and telling people what to do."

"And I'm used to being free, and you have had me trapped for the last few months. I want to be free; I want to choose you, you get that right?" she goes to open the car door, but I stop her, turning her around and kissing her lips, I stay where we are. In this moment, in this time. Me and her.

No fucking others could come between us.

"And no breaking legs." She says as I pull away.

"I don't know what you are talking about." I wink and hold open the door. "I'll take you back to your apartment." I tell her, she gets in, and on the drive, she tells me how she plans to work even after the baby is born. Just not nights. I don't say much because I think I have too much input in her life as it is. She may not want me to speak, so I don't.

And that's a learning curve—for both of us.

————

"Oh, Clinton." I smile at him; he is seated in my office. His leg shaking as one of my men stand at the door. "Did you really think I called you here to give you her?" His taping stops.

"You don't want her," he spits. "I could make use of her."

"She isn't a possession, Clinton." It takes everything in me to not get up and break his legs. "I made a promise to my wife that I would not break any more legs. But you caused her distress, you went behind my back and thought what, you could end our marriage?" I laugh standing.

"She doesn't love you."

"Keep telling yourself that." I tap his shoulder as I reach him, and he flinches.

"If you broke my legs, she would leave you," he says, uncertainty thick in his voice.

"You think?" I ask, squeezing his shoulder.

"My wife would just up and leave?" I question.

"Damn, here I was thinking we had a solid marriage, and I could go around breaking legs of men who think they can stare at *my wife* in ways that they don't deserve."

I release his shoulder, and reach for his hand, he doesn't have time to stop me. I slam his hand on my desk then pick up my heavy ass candle on my desk and slam it onto his fingers. He screams, before I can even look up my employee stuffs a rag in his mouth to muffles his screams.

Clinton tries to pull his hand back, but it's useless really.

I have a hold of it.

I reach for one finger and lift it back; if it's not broken it's about to be.

"You'll stay far away from my wife, won't you Clinton?" when he cries, I bend it back. "Clinton." He nods his head fast, and I bend it back so it breaks for good measure before I let it go, he pulls it to his chest and cradles it. "You can go now Clinton." He stands his back hunched as he leaves.

"Clinton." He stops as my employee blocks the door. "Leave your phone, I saw what you have of her on there." He took photos of when she was asleep when they were an item.

"No."

"Sorry, did I just hear you correctly." I lift the candle and go to walk back over to him. He reaches for his phone with his good hand and drops it to the floor before he turns and reaches for the door, I nod, and my employee moves so he can leave. Then we watch as he runs off crying like the little bitch he is.

CHAPTER 37
LOTTIE

"He's not coming over again, is he?" Emma asks. I haven't told her about the baby yet. I wanted to make sure I was far enough along before we make any announcement, which means I still have weeks to wait.

"Are you really complaining?" I ask her. She crosses her arms over her chest.

"What?"

"The sounds you make with Barry, I mean, doesn't he have his own place?" I argue with her.

"Well, yes, but he's had other women over there and I refuse to go there." She raises a brow in triumph.

The noises that come out of the room would make anyone want to leave the building, I've heard of people who have had great sex before but these two take it to a whole new level, the screaming of his name, the chuckle when she calls him god.

I get the sex is good. I haven't had sex with Whiskey since the night we got back. He comes over, sleeps in my bed with my new mattress I got, leaves before I wake, and that's it.

He calls during the day, and sometimes he even sends me food. He waits for me at the bar when I close up, and he drives me home.

It's weird, this new predicament we are in.

He's always been the one in charge. And now I am not giving him that power.

Though, I am missing his bed.

"You hardly even see Whiskey, I remind her.

"Well, I do, and I'm still on the train of I hate him for you."

"That's so sweet, but not necessary. I'm getting off that train and learning to try to trust him."

"You think he can be trusted?" she asks me.

"Barry, you think he can be trusted?" I ask her.

"Yes, he never blackmailed me." She goes really quiet. "You know he's into some real dark people, I mean he provides security for some of the worse and covers their tracks." I have never once thought of Whiskey as an angel.

Never.

And I know he has a temper. Especially when it comes to men around me.

And that should bother me more, but lately. It doesn't.

I start making myself a sandwich as the door opens, and in walks Barry and Whiskey, Whiskey holds a bag, and I can smell the food automatically. My morning sickness has eased off a bit if I'm careful with what I eat.

Picking up the bread I put it to my mouth.

"Should you be eating that?" I pause confused at Whiskeys words.

"Did you just question what Lottie is eating, who are you?" Emma says to him, but he ignores her.

"It's processed meats," he says directly to me. I give my best what the fuck stare.

"What would you care? Oh, gosh. Please don't tell me he is some clean-eating freak nut. I can't deal! I eat chocolate way too much to deal with that."

I put the sandwich down and wipe my hands on my shorts.

"Ok."

Emma's eyes go wild as she looks at me.

"Did you just agree? Are you in there?" Emma

waves a hand in front of my face. "Don't let him control you like your father does."

"He doesn't," I tell her.

She points to the sandwich. "So, eat it."

"I can't," I tell her.

"Why?"

"Emma, let's go to bed." Barry walks over, and when he does, I look up and know he knows straight away. Whiskey walks over and starts pulling the food out of the bag. I instantly gag and turn to the sink and throw up what I ate earlier.

"I'm not going to bed, what is wrong with you Lottie, you are acting crazy, like some pregnant...." Her words end. I turn the water on and wipe my face. "Are you pregnant?"

"She can't eat processed meats," Whiskey clarifies.

"And why is that?" Emma asks.

"Yes, I am," I confirm.

"Emma." Barry rubs her shoulders as she stands there staring at me.

"So why are you living here?" she asks.

"I need to be sure I *want* to move in with him. I need it to be my choice." She turns to Whiskey.

"And here you are annoying her, pressuring her." She shakes her head. Whiskey says nothing, just continues to plate up the food.

"Emma." I try to calm her down. "I'm having a baby."

"I know," she says, turning back to me. I watch as her eyes soften. "I'm happy for you." Then she starts crying. "I'm more pissed he knew before me." She points to Whiskey. I can't help but laugh at that and pull her in for a cuddle.

"You can be the godmother."

"Do I get a say?" Whiskey asks.

"No," Emma and I say at the same time.

"Seems fair." He says and pushes towards me a soup. "Try thistle, the lady swore by it on an empty stomach."

"We will need a baby's room," Emma says.

"Ummm, let's just slow down on that, for now at least."

"Yes, let's slow down." Whiskey eyes me, I walk over to him and try the soup, when I don't immediately feel sick, I continue. Standing behind me he wraps his hands around me and leans in.

"I missed you."

And I believe him.

————

Two weeks go by fast, and there isn't one night that Whiskey doesn't stay over. He gives me space during the day, and even some nights I don't even see him, but when I wake in the middle of the night to use the bathroom, he is asleep next to me. Crawling out of the bed I relieve myself in the bathroom before I go back to bed. Crawling in, I feel him move.

"When do you plan to come home?" he asks, pulling me into him. I go easily. "You snore less in my bed."

"I don't snore," I remind him. I do, I totally do.

"It's cute, but you snore a lot more here." His hands wrap around me, pulling me in. "Move in with me, please," he says into my hair. "I want my wife in my bed, at our house." Just as he says those words, loud moaning starts. Then banging on the wall, from a bed.

"They are so noisy."

"Well, you know what would fix that?" he asks, his hands roaming my body. I'm already naked so his fingers slide over my bare skin. "If you moved in with me."

"I'll think about it." The banging gets louder, his hands roam lower and lower, I spread my legs as he slips a hand between them.

"Emma, bark." We both freeze at those words that echo through the walls. Then start laughing. I turn around to face Whiskey, I can just make out his eyes. The way they have the perfect wrinkles around them as he stares at me.

"Does my age bother you?" I ask him, not that I think it ever has. But I want to know all the same. His last wife was closer in age to him, than me.

His hand lifts and brushes my hair from my face.

"No," he says with no hesitation. "Does it bother you?"

"I thought it would, but then again, I never really thought much that night I saw you." I smile at him.

"No, I guess neither of us did. It was just need." He leans in and kisses my lips softly his hand staying on my face, when he pulls back, I do to.

"It was…." Before I can even finish my words, I feel my stomach turn, getting up and running to the bathroom the soup I had earlier comes up fast. A hand comes on my back and starts to rub, someone barks. I look up to him, and we both laugh, despite the fact that I am on my hands and knees on the bathroom floor.

"Ok, that was it, the barking, the spew. I'll move in." I tell him. He smiles, stands, and reaches for a wash cloth, I take the opportunity to admire his ass. Because now he sleeps naked too, right next to me.

"I can feel you staring at my ass," he says, and I

can't help but smile at his ass, he wets the cloth and looks over his shoulder at me and winks before he turns and bends down to wipe my mouth. He kisses me on my cheek and then helps me up.

After walking back into the room, he immediately goes to my closet grabs a suitcase and starts packing.

"What are you doing, it's late."

"Fuck that, my wife just said she will come back home. Home is where we are going. The car will be here soon. Get dressed." He looks over his shoulder at me still naked. "I can still feel you staring at my ass."

"You are naked," I say with a wave of the hand towards his very naked body.

"If you don't want to get dressed, put a robe on and you can go straight back to sleep tomorrow. I'll take the day off and we can sleep in."

"Do you do that, take days off?" I ask him reaching for the robe.

"No, but for my wife. I will." He slides on some pants, followed by a shirt, and picks up two suitcases full of my clothes. "We will get the rest tomorrow. Come on wife, let's go."

I didn't think I would give in so early, and I tried to resist. I tried to resist him.

But he is like a magnet, I can't seem to stay away and I only really want to stick to him.

Even though he was an asshole.

Even though he tricked me, manipulated me.

I still want him.

And the best part? He wants me more.

CHAPTER 38
LOTTIE

We're inseparable, and I'm extremely needy. Of him and his time. I want him near me every second of every day. I love him with my whole heart. This man has stolen it and proved himself to me over and over again by constantly showing up, and being there for me better than anyone else has ever been.

I had to stop working. My feet swelled up, and Whiskey wants me to rest, but in doing that I need him more. His company seems to be the only thing that soothes me. Makes me calm when I'm hectic. Because thinking about the impending birth gives me anxiety.

Emma and Barry have moved into the apartment that I shared with Emma, and Whiskey and I are in his apartment, and we rent out the house. I preferred his apartment and its where he always felt more at home in. The baby's room is done and ready right next door to us.

My mother and father have been around more, which comes at a surprise to both Whiskey and me, because if I wanted to see my father before, I had to make arrangements, and now they come over all the time.

Tonight is a celebration for my father's birthday, and I'm struggling with what to wear.

Whiskey finally comes home from work, and his arms immediately wrap around my waist. "How are my beautiful girls?"

"Tired and missing you."

He chuckles in my ear then nips it. "I'll take time off soon, I promise."

I groan as I reach for a red dress that's stretchy enough for my round belly. Handing it to him, he helps me into it, then does it up. He kisses my shoulder before he steps away undoing his tie and replacing it with a red one to match what I'm wearing.

"Do I have to go?" I whine.

Whiskey has been so good. Better than good. I can't get enough of him.

"Yes." He kisses my nose, then grips my hand as we leave.

My mother greets us first, wrapping her arms around me. Then she kisses Whiskey on the cheek before pulling away. She still isn't his biggest fan, but since he has been including them in all appointments with the baby, she has warmed up to him.

My father yells my name with a wine in his hand as he walks his way toward me, then he hugs me. Yeah, he's become a hugger, which I never expected from him. So, I hug him back before he shakes hands with Whiskey.

"Sixty and about to be a grandfather," he says, smirking. "Couldn't be happier." And I believe him when he says that. Because for some reason, I believe he will treat my daughter differently than he treated me. He announced his retirement a few weeks ago, and I can see the heaviness that has lifted now. I see it in my mother as well.

"We found out the sex," Whiskey says, smiling. He pulls out an envelope and hands it to my father. "Happy birthday."

My mother goes to snatch it away, but my father manages to get it first. "Is it in here?"

I nod at his excitement. He turns to my mother. "You can find out after me."

She pokes her lip out as he opens it, and when he does, he smiles, then looks at me. "She's going to be as beautiful as you are."

"A granddaughter?" my mother asks, a tear leaving her eye. I didn't know she could cry. I guess I'm proved wrong.

"The best birthday present ever," my father says as Clinton walks over. I haven't seen him since he told me the truth about Whiskey.

Whiskey straightens when he sees him and grips my back. I told Whiskey it was Clinton who told me, and he hasn't seen him since.

Clinton eyes us and turns and walks the other way.

We mingle, get compliments, and then we leave. It's one of my favorite events because the pressure is gone. And I actually enjoy it.

How my life got to where it is today reads like a fictional novel full of stress and deceit. But in the end, it's worked out. And I got the man who looks at me as if I'm the air he breathes.

What more could I ask for?

His hands touch my body, lifting the dress from me. And a mouth so hot touches my belly, kissing it before we even get to the bedroom.

"In this life, and the next, I would choose you, over and over again."

I grip his head and pull it to my lips. "And I would choose you."

Whiskey lifts me up, big belly and all, and carries me to our bed. He treats me as if I'm fragile, like I could break. Until I'm on top and taking control.

He likes it when I take control.

And as much as I love him, Whiskey stole my heart with blackmail, but what he didn't expect was to love me.

CHAPTER 39
BONUS SCENE
LOTTIE

My leg shakes as we sit at the doctor's office. Whiskey is away for work—he didn't want to go, but he reluctantly did. He tried to get out of it, but I told him I was fine.

I'm not.

I've been sick for weeks. Started off with a food poisoning, then the flu that never ended.

And now.

I'm at the doctor's again, this time with blood results.

"I have to tell him, right?" I say to Emma, biting my lip.

"Yes, and Whiskey thinks you walk on fucking water, so you will be fine." Barry is in the car with

Jacinta, our baby girl, while she sleeps. She is perfect in every sense of the word. She completed us, and I honestly thought I was done. I felt like she was it; we never planned to have any more kids.

"I gotta tell him, but I'll wait to he's home," I say, standing.

"Can you even wait that long? You tell him everything." I do. While I love my relationship with Emma—she's my best friend—Whiskey is my soul mate.

"Sure, I can; he's back tomorrow. I can hold it in."

"So, when he calls and asks how your day went?"

"I'll lie." I smile, stepping outside. We spot Barry in the car, holding Jacinta. She must have woken up. As soon as we reach him, he eyes us over his sunglasses.

"So, are we pregnant again or what?" My mouth hangs open at his words.

"Barry," Emma chides and walks over, taking Jacinta before placing her back into her car seat.

"What? I was joking." He shakes his head before climbing into the back seat.

Emma eyes me but says nothing as we drive off. She and Barry have been doing good, so good, in fact, that he plans to propose to her this week. I'm actually not meant to know, but Whiskey let it slip before he left.

"Ok, so plans this weekend. I need you both to make plans. I have plans."

"Ummm, ok, how many times can you say plans in one sentence?" Emma asks, shaking her head. Barry grips the wheel tighter on our way home, and I smile. He's so nervous.

"Is that Whiskey?" Emma asks, pointing out the window. Sure enough, it is. He's leaning against a pole with one leg kicked up and sunglasses on his eyes as he reads something on his phone. My phone dings, and I look down at the screen.

> Whiskey: Naked, you in our bed.
> Fuck it's all I can think about.

I smile at the text as Barry stops the car. Whiskey looks up and slides his phone into his pocket before he walks around and opens my door. He reaches for me and pulls me into him. I inhale, and when I do, I feel like I am home.

In his arms.

"How are my girls?" He pulls back and brushes

his hand down my face. "Are you feeling better?" I nod, unable to form words. "Good, because I have plans, and they involve you in bed. Naked."

"I saw your text." He smirks and leans down to kiss my lips, hands on either side of my face. The minute his lips touch mine, I melt into him. If I had a wish upon my death, it would be that he could kiss me, like this, while I go.

His tongue slides in as my mouth opens just as Barry says, "Get a room!" He grumbles something else before Whiskey pulls back, and I pout at the loss just before he leans in and bites my bottom lip.

"We have a room, which I intend to use." He pulls away and walks to the car, and I watch him. He's dressed in his suit with slight stubble still on his face from not shaving.

How did I get so lucky?

Barry has hold of Jacinta, and Whiskey takes her from him. She goes happily to her father. Her face lights up, and I wonder, at times, does she love me as much as she loves him?

I'm sure she does.

"Ok, well since you are done with chauffer services, I have places to be, woman. Get in the car so we can go get naked."

"So romantic." Emma laughs with an eye roll,

giving us a wave as she gets in. I carry the baby bag as we walk into our apartment.

"What did the doctor say?" Whiskey asks, placing Jacinta into her highchair. He goes straight to the fridge to grab her yogurt, then, he places a bib on her and looks to me, waiting for an answer. "Bunny?"

"I'm pregnant," I blurt out. "Again," I add.

He stays quiet as he feeds Jacinta, and I don't know what to do. I twiddle my fingers and look down at my feet as I feel him come over to me. He pulls me into his hard body and kisses me again, although, this one isn't an I miss you. This one is an I'm going to devour you. His hands find my ass, and he lifts me up so my legs have to go around his waist. My hands hook around his neck as I pull him even closer and kiss him back. Jacinta makes a noise, and he stops, then he continues kissing me and places his head against my forehead.

"Fuck, the best thing I ever did in this life was forcing you to marry me." I laugh at his words. Even though I thought I hated him back then, I wanted him, too. I never thought our outcome would be like this.

Perfection.

That's how I see us. No one could tear us down

—apart from ourselves—and I highly doubt either of us plan to do that.

We are infatuated with each other and our life.

It just keeps getting better and better.

ABOUT THE AUTHOR

USA Today Best Selling Author T.L. Smith loves to write her characters with flaws so beautiful and dark you can't turn away. Her books have been translated into several languages. If you don't catch up with her in her home state of Queensland, Australia you can usually find her travelling the world, either sitting on a beach in Bali or exploring Alcatraz in San Francisco or walking the streets of New York.

Connect with me tlsmithauthor.com

ALSO BY T.L. SMITH

Sinister Love (Dark Intentions Duet 2)

Cavalier (Crimson Elite #1)

Anguished (Crimson Elite #2)

Conceited (Crimson Elite #3)

Insolent (Crimson Elite #4)

Playette

Love Drunk

Hate Sober

Heartbreak Me (Duet #1)

Heartbreak You (Duet #2)

My Beautiful Poison

My Wicked Heart

My Cruel Lover

Chained Hands

Locked Hearts

Sinful Hands

Shackled Hearts

Reckless Hands

Arranged Hearts

Unlikely Queen

A Villain's Kiss

A Villain's Lies

Moments of Malevolence

<u>Moments of Madness</u>

<u>Moments of Mayhem</u>

Connect with T.L Smith by tlsmithauthor.com

Printed in Great Britain
by Amazon

42321764R00198